XU XI was born in Hong Kong to a Chinese-Indonesian family. The city was home to her until her mid-twenties, after which she led a peripatetic existence around Europe, America and Asia. For eighteen non-consecutive years, the author held a second career in international marketing and management with various multinationals. At the end of 1997, she finally surrendered completely to fiction. She now inhabits the flight path connecting New York, Hong Kong and New Zealand.

The New York Times named her a pioneer writer from Asia in English. "In the 1970's and 1980's, when she was developing her fictional voice, Xu Xi felt alone in her homeland. Unlike most Asian writers here, she wrote in English. Twice, for long periods, her antidote for isolation was to live in the United States." She is an active champion of literature from Asia, and compiled the first comprehensive anthology of Hong Kong writing in English covering prose and poetry from 1945 to the present. There is no question, as *Asiaweek* once said of her work, "that she gets to the heart of the matter." In addition her writing, she also teaches at the MFA program of Vermont College in Montpelier.

Awards include a New York State Arts Foundation fiction fellowship and the *South China Morning Post* story contest winner. She has been a resident writer at the Jack Kerouac Project of Orlando, Florida, Kulturhuset in Bergen, Norway, and the Anderson Center in Red Wing, Minnesota. Her fiction, essays, book reviews and op-eds have been published and broadcast internationally. She holds a MFA in fiction from the University of Massachusetts at Amherst.

Overleaf Hong Kong is her sixth book and the first collection that includes essays. For further information on her work and life, please visit www.xuxiwriter.com.

XU XI's books from Chameleon Press

Hong Kong Rose (2nd ed 2004)

Chinese Walls & Daughters of Hui (2nd ed 2002)

*History's Fiction (*2001)

The Unwalled City (2001)

Other books

*City Voices: Hong Kong Writing in English 1945 to
    the Present,* ed Xu/Ingham (Hong Kong
    University Press, 2003)

OVERLEAF HONG KONG

A Chameleon Press book

OVERLEAF HONG KONG

ISBN 988-97060-6-7

© 2004 Xu Xi (*a.k.a.* S. Komala)

Published by Chameleon Press
23rd Floor, 245-251 Hennessy Road, Hong Kong
www.chameleonpress.com

Distributed in North America by WEATHERHILL
41 Monroe Turnpike, Trumbull, CT 06611
tel 800.437.7840 • *fax* 800.557.5601 • *www.weatherhill.com*

Agent for all rights HAROLD MATSON COMPANY
276 Fifth Avenue, New York, NY 10001 • *hmatsco@aol.com*

Typeset in Adobe Garamond and Optima

Cover design by Image Alpha (Holdings) Ltd.

Printed and bound in Hong Kong by Regal Printing

OVERLEAF HONG KONG

Stories & Essays of the Chinese, Overseas

by

XU XI

Chameleon Press

ACKNOWLEDGEMENTS

These stories and essays (or an earlier version) were originally published as follows:

"Go Parents" in the anthology *Nineteen,* Silverfish Books, Malaysia, 2003, and subsequently in *The Wild East* 5/6, Hong Kong, 2003; "Light of the South" in *Dimsum* 3, Hong Kong, 2000, subsequently in *Great River Review* 33, Minnesota, 2001 and *Frigatezine* 3, www.frigatezine.com, 2001-'02; "The Raining Tree" in *Hawaii Pacific Review* 7, Hawaii, 1992 (Chako); "The Sea Islands" in *Imprint* 2, Hong Kong, 1979 (Komala); "Rubato" in *Echoes,* New York, Spring 1992 and subsequently in *Hawaii Review* 34, Hawaii, 1992 (Chako); "Pineapple Upside Down Bird" in *Brooklyn Free Press,* New York, January 1989 (Chako); "Apollo Kissed Me" in *Fiction Cincinnati,* Ohio, 1986 (Chako); the excerpt from *Wah Kiu* in *Yuan Yang* 2, Hong Kong, 2001; "Wah Kiu Wanderers" in *Asia Magazine,* Hong Kong, March 24-36, 1995 (Chako); "Burnt Out Ambitions" in *Asia Magazine,* Hong Kong, February 2-4, 1996 (Chako); "Multiple Meanings of Being Chinese" in *Rice Paper* 6:3, Canada, 2001; "Rocking the Sampan" in *Rice Paper* 5:1, Canada, 1999; "Words and the Corners of Souls" in *The Asian Wall Street Journal,* Hong Kong, December 24, 1999; "Linguistic Erotica" in *Lit* 3, New York, 2000; "Life as a Colony Rat" in *The Correspondent,* Hong Kong, Winter 2001; "Letter from Hydra, Greece" in *Woman Executive* 10, Hong Kong, 1981 (Komala); "On Compromise" in *Great River Review* 33, an excerpt of the piece titled "Remarks to the Kiwanis", Minnesota, 2001.

The essays "'Home' Is Where We All Might Be" and "America's Face" were originally broadcast on RTHK Radio 3 on December 30, 2001 and November 26, 2002 respectively.

Publications prior to 1996 appeared under Xu Xi's (English) names for Kingsley

CONTENTS

Author's Preface

A great thrill of girlhood was the arrival of overseas cables (or telegrams) for my father. The Cable & Wireless messenger in his pale blue shirt and navy shorts (or slacks in winter) would bicycle up to our doorstep. This was no small feat, because we lived on the seventeenth floor of a building in Tsimshatsui, and I used to picture him raising his bicycle on its back wheel to maneuver it and himself into the tiny lift.

Should Mum be home, there followed a commotion of rummaging in her handbag for a tip. Twenty Hong Kong cents, a virtually worthless amount today, was enough for the dark-skinned "messenger boy," or at least, that was what my mother said. They were almost always dark-skinned Chinese, these suntanned men who were hardly young, but robust and hardy enough to bicycle through the roads of Kowloon, risking limbs and nerves in between double decker buses and mad taxicabs. All to bring us those white envelopes, measuring less than a standard one but larger than a playing card, enclosing urgent missives from Jakarta or Tokyo or London or from wherever out there, that larger, unknown world.

On those envelopes, my father's name and cable address: *Overleaf, Hong Kong.*

The messenger would hand me the envelope, with its perforated receipt slip which, if Mum wasn't home, I would sign and return with the requisite tip. It was a moment that felt adult, important, as if my signature on that line conferred on me a knowledge of that larger world, making it tangible, palpably real. Such self-importance was quickly deflated, however, when I tore open the vertical lines of perforation across the top and removed the single white sheet with its royal blue edges. The words were always incomprehensible, not the actual words themselves but the meaning behind those staccato phrases, broken up by "STOP" where punctuation ought to be. And then I would ring my father at his Ice House Street office in Central to read those messages, including the "stops," and he would make me repeat every word to ensure an accurate transcription. Afterwards would linger a vague feeling of relief at having accomplished this responsible task mingled with disappointment that the larger world still remained a vast, incomprehensible mystery filled with shipments and arrivals, flight numbers and departures, delays and price quotations, a world which I could not yet know, which sometimes felt like a world I would never know.

The sense of knowing but not quite knowing encapsulates the condition of the *wah kiu,* the "Overseas Chinese" that is at the heart of this story and essay collection. Growing up *wah kiu-*Indonesian in Hong Kong, I knew what it felt like to look almost like but not to be Chinese, to speak but not to know the language the way local Cantonese families knew it. In our household was a babble of tongues, a gaggle of arriving and departing relatives and other visitors of all skin colors from abroad. Friends and classmates at my local school, Maryknoll Convent, were either clearly foreign (such as the Portuguese,

Indian or the odd English or American girl) or Chinese. To be betwixt and between was the condition of the handful of us who were odd, incomprehensible, unknowable. The handful shrank as I grew up. Those girls and their families often did not remain, leaving Hong Kong for San Francisco, or Kuala Lumpur, or Manila, or, to what seemed the most romantic destination back in the sixties, Guam. I have since been to the first three cities, but not to Guam. I know it's hardly the island paradise I once imagined. Perhaps I should leave it untrammeled, since that which was imagined provides solace and sustenance, since those imaginings create only separation, but not estrangement.

My father, like many *wah kiu,* was essentially a trader, or "merchant" as he described himself. He traded in manganese ore principally, although in later years he also traded lots of various goods. Trade seems a natural activity for this diaspora; to move things across oceans echoes our own movements, initially out of China, and then onwards to whatever corner of the globe will take us. By the time I was old enough to begin to understand the content of my father's cables, I too descended into the world of trade and commerce. Over the years, I have been employed, variously, at an airline, an airfreight/courier concern, an international business newspaper, thus ensuring the continuation of movement of people and things, all of which is recorded and recalled.

I say "descent" because, as any "real Chinese" or Sinologist knows, in traditional Chinese society the merchant occupies the lowest rung of the social ladder, well below the poet and peasant. As a prose writer, I may not have risen to the heights of the poet, but my rural home bases ensure companionship of the peasantry. But any writer trades in ideas. I know no other way of being, either Chinese or otherwise, except to trade. The global community (and how often do we hear now that we must submit, descend, to "globalization") demands this exchange of people, words, products, this barter of willingness and goodwill. Otherwise we *will* descend even further into a divided and conquered world, where *you* cannot imagine *me* because we separate ourselves by borders – unyielding, impenetrable – whether cultural, racial, religious, ideological, political, sexual, where you cannot be me and I will never be you because we *refuse* to cross the divide, negotiate the peace treaty, compromise or confabulate, because, essentially, we prefer to elevate our own brand of humanity to a self-proclaimed superior state, in order to disparage what we refuse to see and know, what we insist we cannot embrace.

So I trade, and will continue to exchange my ideas and words, in order to remember the first time I was able to imagine another way of life, a human life unlike mine. That knowledge is precious. It is the basis of real humanity, Chinese or otherwise.

XU XI
January 2004
Seacliff, Waikouaiti, New Zealand

STORIES OF THE CHINESE, OVERSEAS

WE ARE ALL CHINESE HERE

GO PARENTS

Only in Wellington were there no sheep near the airport, Henk Go noted as he and his wife Pauline journeyed into Auckland. Sheep dotted the landscape on the road north towards the city, although when it came to sheep, Dunedin was overrun.

This was their last week of a three-week trip to the cities of New Zealand, traveling from south to north.

§

"But what about Christchurch?" Pauline had asked, seven months earlier, when Henk planned the trip from their home in Hong Kong.

"It's too English," he said and confirmed the booking, without Christchurch, that very afternoon. If pressed, Henk would not admit to strong feelings one way or another about

Christchurch, although he had never been fond of the former colonial government of their adopted home city. It was just that the travel brochure named Otago "the paradise of the south," which made Dunedin the logical destination. One paradise a trip was quite enough.

Pauline felt a twinge of annoyance. She had *heard* of Christchurch, but not Dunedin. This was *exactly* like years ago when he left out Oxford — where she wanted to visit her English teacher who had retired after years of teaching in Asia — and made her ride that uncomfortable train to Edinburgh instead! She should perhaps take more initiative in planning trips, as Julia, their younger daughter often urged. She wasn't like her daughters though, both of whom had Important Jobs with secretaries and assistants; Pauline was a month away from seventy eight.

Minutes later, she remembered that she hadn't told the maid what to cook for dinner. Christchurch vanished, a forgotten notion in the scheme of her days.

§

"This is a very nice hotel room," Pauline remarked as she looked out at the harbor. Picking up a tent card, she read aloud. "The City of Sails. I wonder why they call it that."

Henk began unpacking. Once, he might have snapped at Pauline, wondering *how* she could be so ignorant. Hadn't she heard, didn't she know, the races, boats, world famous. *World famous.* Nowadays, he preferred to conserve energy. At seventy seven, he was too old to educate her any longer if she wouldn't retain anything.

Pauline asked. "What's the itinerary for today?"

"In the folder."

What folder, she wondered. Why did he always have to be so short tempered? While rummaging in the carry on, Pauline recalled Johnson, their youngest child and only son saying, as he and his wife drove them to the Minneapolis airport two years ago, *Mum, will you please stop asking what time the flight is?* His tone, like Henk's.

She unfolded the four page itinerary. Henk had crossed off each item as their trip progressed, followed by comments like "so-so,""interesting," and "guide impossible to understand." The last was next to Lanarch Castle. Where was that? Wellington? Pauline wracked her brain but simply couldn't remember. Her memory was dreadful these days, although she wished her family were more understanding since what, after all, could she do about age? At least Julia was patient, only why did she have to live so far away, in London of all places, to which Henk refused to go?

Putting away the itinerary — it made her brain reel — she said. "Can we not eat lamb tonight?"

"Eat what you like."

"Yes but what I meant was don't choose a place that specializes in lamb."

"You don't have to order lamb," he said, wishing she would simply come to the point. Unlike him, his wife had never cared for the taste of mutton or lamb, or even goat.

"But there's not much choice if we don't go to a restaurant that offers more variety."

"What do you expect here? You're the one who wanted to come to New Zealand."

Pauline felt her frustration mount. *He* was the overweight one, with high cholesterol and blood pressure, not her.

"But . . ."

Henk, however, had gone into the bathroom and closed the door.

§

Eight months earlier, Henk had declared at breakfast. "I want to go to South America before I die." He laid down the *South China Morning Post.* On page four was an advertisement for an Argentinian tango performance.

"Ie-Yan, *kelar,*" Pauline shouted at their maid, who popped out of the kitchen to clear the table. Ie-Yan spoke only Javanese, Henk and Pauline's native Indonesian dialect, and came from Tjilatjap, Pauline's home village in Central Java. This arrangement riled Jeannie, their eldest, the only child who still lived in Hong Kong, although outside the city on Lantau Island in a village by the beach. Jeannie insisted it was easy to get there, now that the airport was on the island and connected by mass transit, although her mother remained unconvinced. *Mum, why don't you hire a Filipino,* she demanded. *That way at least she'd speak English, and many speak Cantonese as well. You shouldn't have to go food marketing with Ie-Yan because she can't converse. A "domestic helper" shouldn't be helpless!* None of the Go children spoke Indonesian, having all been born and raised in Hong Kong.

Over the clatter of dishes, Henk continued. "We should go during January, after everyone's done with Christmas vacations. There are plenty of deals then. What do you think?" It upset Henk that he must ask, because the money wasn't his, although Pauline usually claimed it was for both of them to use. He had to admit she was good, though, agreeing to spend the inheritance from her eldest brother on travel. For the last three years, life held the promise of excitement once more.

"Don't talk about dying."

"Why not? It's the only thing we can't know."

Pauline didn't know what to say to his cryptic comments. They upset her. Back when they were courting, Henk *never* said things like that, wanting only to please her, taking her to the cinema, bringing flowers he could then ill afford, promising she would "never have to lift a finger at home or go to work again" if she married him. It had been *years*, decades since he'd taken her to the cinema.

She ventured. "Isn't South America unstable?"

He snorted. "Argentina's fine." This was over a year before the peso was flung out to free float in the ocean of global exchange.

Argentina! All Pauline could conjure up were *gauchoes* and alfalfa — from her children's primary school geography textbooks — neither of which held much appeal. Plus a *horribly* long flight. Henk, she suspected, was attracted by beef, so bad for his heart. There already was an Argentinian steak house in Hong Kong so why did they have to fly halfway round the world to eat? Stubborn was what he was.

In desperation, she said the first thing that came into her head. "What about New Zealand? My niece Marissa's in Auckland." Last night, Julia had been chatty on the phone, although the only thing Pauline remembered of their conversation was, *did you know, Mum, New Zealand was the first country where women got the vote?*

"That's a ridiculous idea!" Henk exclaimed.

Pauline choked and left the table. This time, her husband's silence lasted two days before he relented.

"Your father's impossible," Pauline complained over the phone to an exasperated Jeannie for the third time during her forty-eight hour exile. "I *begged* him to explain why South America. Just explain is all I ask. But no, he pretends to be reading, *refusing* to say a word. Your father is so unreasonable. I should have left him years ago!"

Jeannie, who was running to a business meeting, registered only the last, tediously familiar sentence. "A bit late, Mum, don't you think? Besides, what's the fuss? You don't plan any travel and go where he wants anyway."

"You always take your father's side . . . !"

"Got to work. Later, Mater." It was a minor triumph for Jeannie, who suffered Pauline hanging up on her abruptly, inexplicably, in the middle of numerous conversations. *Utter fruitcakes, both of them,* she later emailed her siblings to apprise them of their parents' latest travel plans. *South America will never be the same.*

§

On board the ferry from Auckland for Waiheke Island, Henk marveled at the easy climate and lack of crowds. Refreshing, although the city life wasn't very stimulating. This was a young country though, like the U.S., so a bland and immature culture was inevitable, given the absence of history. Even as the thought formed, he recalled, uncomfortably, the time he echoed this sentiment to Johnson and his American wife.

They rolled their eyes at each other, thinking he wouldn't notice, but had not contradicted him.

Their guide was explaining schedule options for the return boat ride.

"We have to be back by three," Pauline said.

"Why?"

"Marissa is picking us up at 3:15." When he didn't respond she added, "I told you she was. She's taking time off work to drive us around this afternoon, specially."

Henk turned and gazed at the water. Irritating, having to hurry back, yet clearly, there wasn't any choice.

Pauline hovered. "Henk, please say something. We will go back in time, won't we?"

He did not turn around. "What do you want me to say?"

Pauline's heart sank. This whole trip was a huge mistake. Wasn't it enough that she let him spend her money — and Henk never chose economy when an expensive option was available — risking their future, all for the sake of pleasure? *He* was the one who insisted on traveling. And now, when they went where she wanted for once, mostly because she had heeded Julia's insistence to take initiative and make some changes, he was deliberately going to spoil everything.

All this energy, wasted, for what? Beautiful scenery, yes, but what use was beauty if things simply never changed? Her daughter meant well but she didn't understand. Pauline gripped the handrail, forcing herself to extract what pleasure she could from the last days of their trip.

§

During the three weeks before he gave into Pauline's wish to visit New Zealand, Henk read every word of the brochures from his travel agent, plus all the literature he personally acquired from the consulates and airlines of South American nations.

South America. The name lolled in Henk Go's mind.

Jeannie bought him a video of *The Tango Lesson*, saying, *I know, I know, "Dad only watches documentaries." Try, just try this movie. You might even learn something for a change. It's better than all that travel crap you're reading*. The video sat by the television, unwatched, until the night Pauline complained, loudly, over dinner, that the only reason he wanted to go to South America was to upset her. He refrained from saying, *but it's the last continent*, knowing she probably wouldn't remember, or care.

Pauline fell asleep ten minutes into the movie, the way she did, every night, no matter what was on television. Henk continued watching, fascinated by the passion of the dance, surprised it didn't bore him as he expected it would. Two thirds of the way through, he suddenly thought that about the only thing he and his wife had ever agreed on, in over forty years together, was the naming of all their children "J's," a decision arrived at in an intoxicated duet of laughter and whimsy, the night she agreed to marry him.

§

Back before Henk's bankruptcy in '64, when his business brought in millions, he had taken Pauline around the world. Twice. First class. He had never been prouder of anything in his life. Virtually every major city in North America, Africa, Europe, and Australia that was not closed to them during the late fifties and early sixties. Their Indonesian passports precluded Israel and, of course, China. This last restriction was *a gross absurdity,* he complained often over the years. *We're still Chinese, aren't we? Being "overseas" shouldn't be held against us! Our ancestors came from the same motherland after all.* Pauline had never bothered arguing this point; why "waste saliva" complaining about something that didn't really matter, and more important, couldn't be changed?

The first trip charted the path of Taipei, New York, Casablanca, London, Sydney, and the second trip, Singapore, Canberra, San Francisco, Athens, Johannesburg. There were many other cities along those routes. South America was reserved for a third and separate trip that never happened. When Pauline asked, *why separate,* he dismissed her question as illogical. Truthfully, he had been a bit afraid, back then, although he couldn't admit that. More important, there was some knowledge that eluded him, unlike other places about which the more he read, the more he felt he knew.

Of all the continents, South America seemed the most distant adventure, where a pulse, not a place, lay at the end of the journey, and where money offered no passport to discovery. He didn't know how to say this to Pauline or anyone.

Henk kept one postcard from each city in a scrapbook, arranged in the order of their itinerary, labeled with the names of their hotels and the major sights, recording also the air miles between destinations. "The facts of the world" he called them. Every year, Pauline sent Christmas cards to the people they met on those trips, none of whom they ever saw again, since travel had been unaffordable for some thirty years afterwards, the priority being, always, survival and the children. Economy class travel, like Henk's business, resumed slowly as time passed. In 1997, they even visited China. No trip, however, was quite like those first, two, astonishing ones when everything was unknown, money no obstacle, and time still their slave.

The three Go siblings poured through this scrapbook incessantly throughout their childhood, begging to be told — *again, more* — the stories of these trips. Their parents obliged readily. Jeannie (a graphic designer) drew creative variations of the flight paths; Julia (a market analyst) memorized and updated the facts of the world, checking the annual reports of cities in the library, even writing to hotels to make sure they still existed; Johnson (a city budget administrator) re-attached the postcards as the rice glue dried and flaked. For the last five years, Johnson's wife Elaine had taken over sending the annual greetings, because Pauline's arthritis made writing cards too painful. Elaine recorded the addresses exactly the way her mother-in-law wished, noting who had died or otherwise vanished.

As adults, all three children have a surplus of frequent flyer miles.

§

Following Jeannie's email, Julia urged her mother to stand firm, saying she could always go to New Zealand on her own by joining a tour, to which Pauline replied, *How can, and leave your father alone?* Julia curbed impatience, and tried to say, nicely, *but if you'd just express what you really want for a change,* which only unleashed the usual *"you have no idea, you just don't know your father"* tirade.

Johnson, who wouldn't take sides, suggested to both parents during his weekly call home that they come visit their two grandchildren in Minneapolis instead. *Uh, impossible,* said Henk, although he failed to say why. *So cold,* Pauline said, adding, *too much trouble for Jane,* to which Johnson sighed and said, for what had to be the hundredth time, *Mum, my wife's name is Elaine, not Jane,* Jane being the child before Jeannie who died at age two. Elaine no longer got upset over her mother-in-law's persistent error. Even Johnson, the most diplomatic of the three, was beginning to give up any hope for sanity, as he said in his email to his sisters that night.

When Henk continued to research South America, Jeannie emailed her siblings, *I told you so, they always do what Dad wants.* Jeannie got away with such smugness only because she was oldest.

§

"You're not going to die!" Pauline finally yelled at Henk. Three weeks of watching him lust over brochures and photos of South America had been more than she could bear. "And I won't go to South America."

"*Hoosh,*" he said, glancing at the closed bedroom door. "The servant will hear you." It was late and Ie-Yang was already in bed.

Tears welled up in Pauline's eyes. "I refuse to spend anymore money traveling only to where you want to go. All you want to do is spend. Didn't you learn your lesson in '64? If I hadn't dismissed all our servants, economized *and* gone back to work, even though you objected, where would we be now? Where?"

"Stop crying. I'm not insisting on anything."

"Then we'll go to New Zealand." She saw the twitch of his lips, prelude to a protest, and declared. "It's *my* money."

He went silent. Then. "Fine. You know, though, it is in the middle of nowhere. The flight's long, and we can't stop in the U.S. first to see Johnson and Elaine and the grandkids."

He spread open the atlas, knowing it hadn't occurred to her till that moment exactly where the country was in relation to the rest of the world. She glared at the page, fighting off hesitation, her face glowering with passion.

"I don't care," she said at last. "Johnson's bringing the whole family here this summer. He *promised*. Also, we'll fly business class. The children won't mind. And we'll only stay in five-star hotels!"

Henk laughed, knowing he'd lost. If nothing else, this would get him closest to, if not actually on Antartica, the only continent he did not feel compelled to visit.

It wasn't, as Henk would later tell Jeannie in person, privately, after New Zealand was booked, because it was their mother's money, but because it was high time Pauline made a decision.

Jeannie, annoyed, countered, *you guys don't have any money worries now and she only has to pay for the land part so what's the big deal?* The children were floating the tickets, as they had other trips, with mileage. *Besides, Mum doesn't even like that idiot cousin of ours,* meaning Marissa in Auckland, *and doesn't know the difference between New Zealand and, and, oh I don't know. . . new potatoes! And on top of it all, she hates lamb, loathes it. It just doesn't make any sense to go there.*

Henk stifled a laugh, knowing Jeannie wasn't entirely wrong, but when it came to Pauline, Jeannie was unreasonable and overwrought — this petulant girl who hadn't quite grown up — although there were times he felt she really ought to know better and be more forgiving towards her mother, she being the eldest and all.

What he didn't dare say to Jeannie was that this might well be his and Pauline's last trip together. His health, he knew, was deteriorating. Despite her bravado, his daughter was easily frightened. He had never known how to reassure his children about much, least of all about fate, to which Jeannie, especially, would only retort that he was being "too Chinese-fatalistic." Henk had never been quite certain what his daughter meant by this.

§

The walk to the beach was longer than Pauline expected, and she regretted, now, her insistence that they do this. Surprisingly, Henk hadn't complained, neither about the long car ride — it was comfortable enough but he was never satisfied with anything she planned — nor about having to walk, which was harder on him than her, she being in much better health since he insisted on eating so much red meat, even at his age, despite all her warnings.

He stared silently at the swath of sand and sea and she wondered, would she *ever* know what he was thinking?

"Like Tjilatjap," he said, out of the blue.

Startled, Pauline asked. "What made you think of that?"

"Black sand."

The earth glistened.

"I'm getting blind in my old age," she told their chauffeur-guide, laughing. "I didn't even notice."

Henk said. "This coast, volcanic. Like Tjilatjap."

Later, when their guide took a cigarette break, leaving them alone, Henk said. "Do you remember? On the beach?"

Pauline stared blankly at him. What was her husband on about?

"Don't you?" he persisted. "When I proposed properly, in Tjilatjap, the way you wanted?" He looked hard into her eyes, marveling at that still-gentle face, creased over the years by too many unasked questions.

Then, it came back to her, with startling clarity, their very first trip together.

Three months after they met in Hong Kong, Henk had declared, "I want to marry you."

When Japan ended its Southeast Asian occupation and surrendered to the Allies, the city signaled opportunity, attracting folks like themselves, the *wah kiu,* the "overseas Chinese" as The People's Republic of China officially labeled this emigrant citizenry, politically separate but taxed with culture, history and guilt. Pauline's eldest brother and only relative in Hong Kong had judged this Henk Go unfavorably. He was a doctor and suspicious of men in "business," especially in that post-war, beyond-Mao, still-colonial time, when kings were cabbages and mavericks overran the free world.

She thought over the situation for three weeks, and finally said, he must ask her father, in person, because that was the only way. He found the money — how she never learned — for their Garuda tickets, arranging everything to give her "face" before her parents who were wary of this stranger, not from their village and worse, from a family without sufficient standing and of dubious Chinese blood, unlike her own. Six generations earlier upon arriving from China, Go men had intermarried Javanese women, though their descendants' name and general appearance were still Chinese.

When her father finally said — "it's up to Pauline," thereby making clear his displeasure, even while unable to deny his favorite child's desire — she brought Henk to the black sand beach at night where she laughed at the champagne he dared to bring, wondering, *who had he bribed to get that here?* They drank the magical foreign liquid out of gourd shells, scavenged from the sand, and she said, *yes, now I'll marry you,* because what else could she say to all that love going wild inside her, blood be damned?

Henk repeated, uncertainly. "*Don't* you remember?"

Pauline looked at this man, her husband of almost fifty years, and, pleased that these moments could still come to pass, moments when she saw his mind — in technicolor, unfaded, on a big screen — replied. "Of course I remember. How could I ever forget?"

§

The one thing about New Zealand, unlike any place Henk ever experienced before, was how its gentle face belied a wild heart. Here they were, on a remote and savage beach, yet only forty minutes from the city center.

He faced the Tasman Sea, where land stretched empty along

the western coastline.

Pauline was asking their guide. "This beach is the one, right?"

"What one?" Henk wanted to know.

"The beach where *The Piano* was filmed."

He puzzled, what was his wife talking about? During their travels, she rarely posed questions that presupposed prior knowledge about places, although she asked about flowers and plants they saw.

The guide replied in the affirmative and then suggested they walk a little before heading back, and excused himself to smoke.

When Pauline organized this part of their trip, arranging a private guide and car to take them out to the "countryside" as she called it, Henk felt mildly undermined. The guide handed him a walking stick for the rocky path and he bristled, but Pauline snapped, *take it for goodness sake, it's easier on your leg,* and he capitulated, because the flutter in his heart, at that moment, gave him pause.

Under this late afternoon sunlight, the beauty made up for his earlier annoyance.

Pauline said. "Out here, so startling."

"What film was that?"

"You mean *The Piano?*"

"Yes, yes, what did you think I meant?"

"Don't be so grumpy. Julia took me to the cinema one afternoon when she was home last and we saw it together. Some of it was filmed here."

"What was it about?"

"Something about a piano."

He refrained from rolling his eyes.

"Anyway," she continued, unfazed, "a movie happened on this beach. And, oh yes, the film director was a woman from this country. Imagine. Isn't that something?"

"I suppose," he said, but was more impressed that she remembered. Somehow, it mollified him, knowing that the trip had some purpose for her.

That night, when Pauline fell asleep, as she invariably did, before him, Henk wondered if South America, judging by the photographs he'd seen, would have been too overwhelming, perhaps even beyond his ken.

They would leave New Zealand tomorrow. It hadn't been the most exciting of trips, but it hadn't disappointed him either. The scenery was astounding, and the lamb, and even the beef, had been delicious.

In the bathroom, Henk experienced a short, sharp pain. Heart? The palpitations paused for an instant. Probably nothing, he decided, and suddenly recalled *The Tango Lesson* and the girl's face as she danced, lost to the rhythm. And then found himself thinking, just seconds before his heart gave way, *was it a woman or man who directed that,* and realized, with an odd feeling he couldn't explain, that he simply didn't know.

LIGHT OF THE SOUTH

The first time Viola saw Shibata, he was in the uniform of what she supposed was the *Kempeitai*. A tall, broad shouldered man, with a shock of white hair and a serious, unchanging expression.

"This house belongs to Japan now," was all he said before his men entered.

Viola stared at the men who barely gave her a second glance. They began, methodically, setting up camp in the living room. Shibata headed upstairs towards the master bedroom. Viola followed. He stopped at her bedroom next door.

"Where is your father?"

"This is my uncle's house. My father lives in Indonesia."

He narrowed his eyes. "Then you're not from Singapore?"

"No."

"Where is your uncle and his family?"

"I don't know." Viola wondered why she wasn't more afraid. It had been two days since the morning she'd awakened and found the house deserted. She hadn't gone out after that. Today, the Japanese finally arrived to occupy, the way her cousin Joseph had predicted.

Shibata rubbed his nose, thinking, she must be very young. A problem, her presence. Simpler to kill her right away. "Why are you in Singapore?"

"I attend boarding school. The Convent of the Holy Infant Jesus."

Fourteen, fifteen at most. "You stay in your room," he commanded.

"All the time?"

Her manner, defiant and provocative, tested his patience. "You will ask permission when you want to come out."

Viola loitered at the entrance of her room. "Must I shut the door?"

For a moment, he wanted to slap her mouth. But her smile, nervously mischievous. Shibata relented. She was only a girl after all, too daring for her own good. "You may shut it or leave it open, as you wish."

"Then," she declared. "I will shut it."

§

At dusk, the house was beautiful. Shibata wandered through its rooms. The fragrance of frangipani from the garden permeated the air, lingering in its sensual promise. There were two floors, with wide, sheltered verandahs on each level. A large, rambling structure, almost a mansion.

He ventured into the garden, where the lawn descended down a slope. Mango trees and hibiscus bushes ranged along its borders.

The house, number eleven Toh Crescent, stood at the end of a short cul-de-sac. From the street, the walls surrounding the property and the profusion of growth in the garden kept it out of sight of prying eyes. As a commandant of the *Kempeitai,* the secret police, Shibata had identified it as a useful operating base, because it was near Changi prison where most of the POW's were held. The owners were wealthy Chinese; everything in the house was in good repair. There were keys to the locks of all the doors. With its numerous rooms, it would serve as a holding place for interrogations.

A flickering light in the upstairs window suddenly extinguished itself. He caught sight of the girl's silhouette, frozen in a pose of blowing out a candle. Why was she lighting candles?

But his attention was distracted by one of his men signaling to him from the house.

§

Two more days passed. Viola guessed her uncle and his family had either escaped or were dead. Fear, wound in a tight knot inside, slackened. Even the screams from various rooms in the house had become a routine of startling solos, punctuating the silence. Last night, when a man's cry from directly below had awakened her, she sat up, saw that her own door remained closed, and forced herself back to sleep.

A knock on her door. She glanced at the clock on her dresser. Too early for dinner.

Shibata stood in the doorway. He was not in uniform. In his *yukata,* he looked far less severe.

"You will come for a walk," he said.

She had stepped back and stood by her bed. "And if I don't want to?"

"You don't have a choice."

He waited, staring hard at her. Viola looked out the window. Evening breezes caressed her face. Respite after the rains.

"I have to put on my shoes," she said. "The grass is still wet."

He led her towards the front gate. For one wild moment, Viola wanted to run, as far and fast as she could, before they executed her. If she were sudden and swift enough, she might even escape. But the eerie quiet of the street intimidated. You'll be safe at our house, her uncle had told her when she came to stay. She had felt protected, untouched by the invisible war beyond their boundaries, glad to be away from the empty convent.

"I regret to inform you . . ." Shibata's voice pierced her daydream. "Your uncle has been taken as a prisoner of war." He leaned against the gate, watching for her reaction.

She wanted to ask — And will you execute him? And my cousins and aunt as well? But she asked nothing.

"Do you know who I am? Do you know why we're here?"

She nodded.

"Then you understand?"

She stood about three feet away from him, her back to the house. He continued to watch her, wondering just how much she did understand. She was such a quiet girl, never asking for anything. But that flicker of defiance in her eyes. Dangerous. Impossible to trust the emotions of the young.

"You may go back to the house now."

She turned and slowly climbed the slope.

§

The next morning, her door was open for the first time. Shibata saw that she was wearing a red dress. Previously, she had worn pale colors or white which faded against her fair skin. The bright red illuminated her. And she seemed happy, as if it were her birthday, or some special occasion.

"Will you walk with me again this evening?" She had sought him out deliberately.

"Why?"

"Because I want you to tell me about Japan."

"You don't have to wait till evening. Ask me now."

"I don't wish to."

Defiance flickered, then faded. She seemed suddenly older, like a woman who no longer accepts flattery, who is beyond courtship. "As you wish."

Viola went round to the back of the house, watched by a guard. There was a hiding hole there, one that was difficult to see. It was past the clean kitchen, outside the dirty one that only the servants used. This deep hole could be reached by crawling under a landing. Joseph said a nest of poisonous snakes lived in it.

She stood on the landing and gazed at the sanctuary.

§

When he came to get her for their walk, she made him wait

while she slung a light cardigan over her shoulders the way her aunt used to. It was a semi-conscious gesture, a way of not forgetting. School life, her family in Indonesia, everything was fading as if life before now never existed. Every night, she put a pillow over her head to shut out the screams of people she didn't see.

"You look like a young lady, for a change."

She gave him a half smile. "How do I usually look?"

"Like a girl."

They walked in silence to the front gate. He opened it. She inhaled a frangipani-scented breeze.

"Teach me Japanese."

An unexpected request, it made him smile. He pointed to the frangipani tree at the entrance. "*Kore-wa kirei-de su.* This is pretty."

She solemnly repeated what he said, and then asked, "How do you count numbers?"

He was back in Paris as a music student remembering On-Lan, the Chinese girl who studied with him under the same master that year. They would speak in French or broken English. She had also asked to learn Japanese. But that was over forty years ago when he had been only slightly older than this girl. "Itchy knee," he said, and pretended to scratch his knee.

"Did a mosquito bite you?"

Her serious expression, her look of such concern overcame him. He roared with laughter, his first real laughter since the start of this bloody war. "No, no," he said, wiping the tears from his eyes. "That's the way we count. One, *ichi.* Two, *ni.*"

His laughter subsided.

She seemed unimpressed and lapsed into a thoughtful silence. Then. "You call Singapore *Syonan-To.*"

It sounded like an accusation. "That's the Japanese name."

"What does it mean?"

"Light of the south."

"How beautiful."

For once, she did not look like a hunted animal. He led her along the path towards the cul de sac. She fell in beside him. He talked about his year in Paris. She listened quietly, her face radiant. Time disappeared. Long unheard melodies of youth embraced his senses.

As they circled back to the gate, he asked, "There's a piano in this house. Do you play?"

"Yes."

"You will play for me?"

"Are you ordering me?"

Her voice resonated pain. He wanted to protect her. "No. I am requesting you to do me this honor."

Viola went silent. He tried to read her feelings, but her face betrayed nothing. And then, unexpectedly, a plea flickered in her eyes. "I can't," she said abruptly, and ran back up the path into the house.

§

As soon as her room door was shut, she wept.

At school, they had heard stories of Chinese men taken away and tortured, while women were forced into slavery, or worse. Survival meant surrender. Several girls stashed rat poison under their mattresses, in case Japanese soldiers forced their way inside the convent school gates. The girls cried every night, praying to be sent for, to be released into the safety of their families. Viola would not cry; she refused to believe in this destructive force unleashed on her world.

Surely God had made a mistake.

Every night at the convent, she had lit a candle in a private novena to the Infant Jesus. She resolved to repeat the cycle until He intervened to fix His Father's mistake, and put aside the prayers for her own release. Her schoolmates departed rapidly during those days, sometimes several within an hour. For awhile, it seemed her pleas were heard.

She dried her eyes. Why need she cry now?

Viola lit a candle, beginning the second cycle.

If she were truly brave, like her uncle, she would have fought the Japanese. But dreaming of victories did not stifle fear.

Shibata awoke to a scream from her room that night. He sat up, startled. His prisoners' cries never disturbed the way hers did.

§

"How long will you hold me here?"

She had presented herself, without warning, at his desk. Shibata saw it was just past noon.

"It's almost time for lunch. Why don't you eat with me?" He smiled.

She was wearing the red dress again. A thin girl, with barely formed breasts. He wanted to ask if she had had a nightmare. But she had drawn back into herself.

"You must be hungry. You didn't come to breakfast."

"I wasn't hungry this morning." She stared at the floor. Without looking up, she repeated, "how long will you hold me here?"

"As long as necessary." His tone of voice dismissed her.

She walked away towards the kitchen. A song from school echoed. "*There is a convent school far, far away / Where they eat rotten eggs ten times a day. / Oh, how the children yell / When they hear the dinner bell. / Oh, how the eggs stink miles, miles away.*"

Kitchen smells teased Viola's nostrils. Fish again. She grimaced. She hated fish, despised it. She would rather eat rotten eggs.

§

If only her mother hadn't been too ill to send for her! But Mother was often unwell.

She had been the last boarder. Mother Superior had been kind, and promised she could stay inside the convent with the nuns as long as necessary. Viola was afraid, alone in Singapore, and wanted to go back to Indonesia.

But she kept her resolve, and continued offering her novena, hoping God would see the error of his ways.

Finally, Mother Superior called her uncle, her mother's brother, because the nuns did not dare keep her any longer in the convent in the city's center. Her uncle told her it was already too dangerous to travel home, and that it would be safer to stay at his house.

A knock on her bedroom door.

"Miss Viola to come downstairs." The guard stared unblinkingly at her.

He led her to the west wing, which had been cordoned off since the Japanese occupation.

Shibata was seated in one of the guest bedrooms at a makeshift desk. The bed and dresser that used to be in the room were no longer there. There was a bamboo mat on the floor in front of the desk.

"You're Catholic?" he asked without his usual preamble.

"Yes."

"Then kneel."

She did not flinch even a split second. "No."

"I am ordering you."

"This is not a church." She remained standing, hands by her side. Her pale blue dress hung to her knees. "I only kneel for God."

A difficult girl. Stubborn and proud. Unafraid.

He had to dispense with her.

Why had she been left in the house, in Singapore? It seemed even she didn't know. She would be a problem later when she remembered what she'd seen and heard. The power of youth.

Yet On-Lan's face, On-Lan's thin body. An apparition wavering around this girl.

"Go back to your room," he commanded.

As she left, she pulled her arm away from the guard.

§

Memory could not be more absurd!

All evening, Shibata paced the garden. Frangipanis were in full bloom. Wild fragrances assaulted him. When his second-in-command stopped by, to advise that the one in the back room had finally expired, he barely heard him. He had to do something about that girl. Soon.

The first time he kissed On-Lan, she told him it would only lead to unnecessary complications. He protested, but she wouldn't relent. She infuriated and excited him.

From her window, Viola watched the rays of the setting sun light the garden and house. The grass and bushes badly needed trimming.

She had to pray.

Kneeling by the window, she tried to remember Indonesia. It wasn't true when her cousin said that she got sent to boarding school because her mother didn't want her. Her family hadn't abandoned her because they didn't love her. It had to be the Japanese. Surely they were to blame. Mother Superior had promised: keep the faith and God will love you and always be your protector. But try as she would, her prayers and memories disappeared, unreachable.

She did not light a candle that evening.

Night fell over the garden, shrouding its unruly growth.

§

He slept fitfully all night, awakening at the slightest sound. This was Paris again. A year of freedom before surrendering to duty.

That girl. An irritant, an unnecessary presence. Even his second-in-command was beginning to wonder.

In the morning, Shibata sent for her. He stood up when she entered, and dismissed the guard. "You know what I have to do."

Viola glared at him. She was wearing her red dress.

He couldn't look at her. "You are a prisoner of war," he

declared.

Fear, a tightened vise that could turn no further, snapped. "I hate you," she said, evenly.

It was as if she'd slapped his face. "Prisoner of war," he repeated.

"I hate all of you."

On-Lan's lips, close to his, resistant yet pliant.

He faced her.

Their eyes locked in embrace.

THE RAINING TREE
Conversations with a Chinese Ghost

The tree longs for calm but the wind does not cease.
(Chinese military proverb)

It is evening now. I can still see the tree out there at the end of the path. The raining tree. I wonder if it still rains.

You didn't think I'd come home, did you, Granny? Well, I did. I always loved Port Dickson, and this house. It seems a shame it's got to come down, to make way for some hotel. I don't know where I'll go after I give them the house tomorrow. I suppose I'll go back to Singapore, go back to work.

Let me close the windows for you. What a dreadful storm. Look, our poor tree's shaking. There'll be buds all over the path tomorrow. You wouldn't think, would you, that one tree could afford to lose so many buds? There, much quieter with the window shut, don't you think? We'll sleep better this way.

Oh granny, I don't want them to take away the house. I

know it has to be done, but I still wish . . . oh never mind. I'm sorry. I didn't mean to be cross. It just seems unfair. You should understand. You wouldn't let anyone take our tree away.

Why do you say the tree's different? If anything, the house should be more important than a stupid tree. You're always saying the tree's so important. Sometimes, I don't understand you at all, grandma.

Raining Tree. What a funny name. Trees don't rain. She said this tree could. How crazy. I guess she meant well.

It does sort of rain, though. They must have thought I was crazy when I tried to describe it. I've always called it a raining tee, even if that is a childish name. I should have known they wouldn't understand. Why didn't I keep my mouth shut?

This is a bad storm. I really ought to shut the windows.

Remember the walks we used to take on the beach? Two miles of black sand. I'd like to go on those walks again. I'm sure there isn't a nicer sea than here.

Of course, I remember! I ran, all the way down to the beach. And you kept falling and running, trying to catch me. I was naughty that time. But I was a good girl most of the time, wasn't I? You said I was.

Why did you scare me so much? You did, you know. The night Mum and Dad crashed you wouldn't let me go to the car. You said horrible things about their bodies. You told me not to cry over them, because their ghosts would come back and eat me if I did. That was the night you told me about the tree. You said the tree ghost would do my crying for me, if I'd let it. Granny, you were scary when I was five.

Oh granny, don't cry now. I just wanted to tell you that a tree can't do my crying for me forever.

I must sit down. Last night's show wore me out. They're all almost too friendly to me. Have to be, don't they? I know I'm worth more money than any other model in Singapore. I heard the boss telling that to the top client the other day. Of course I am! They don't really think I'm going to be even tempered and smiling all the time, just for the fun of it, do they? Gosh, I wonder what they'd do if they knew what I actually thought of them?

I'm surprised to see the old house in good shape. I imagined it would have fallen apart by now. The outer staircase felt rickety when I stepped on it this afternoon.

Everything looks fine in here. Well, maybe the mirror's a little rusty around the edges, and those chairs could stand reupholstering . . . what am I worrying for? This place won't be mine anymore tomorrow.

I feel as if I belong here. This room reminds me of my Singapore flat. Safe. Away from the crowds. Why did I come back? The agent could've handled the entire sale for me.

Why do I think about belonging all the time? Stupid idea. No wonder the boss laughed when I asked whether or not I really belonged to the agency. I even asked Neil, the English photographer, whether or not he thought I was beautiful enough to belong to the agency. For no reason at all, right out of the blue I asked him. They must think me silly.

I wonder if they think I'm awfully stuck up because I don't say much? I can't help that. I think they're too nosey in Singapore. Always asking questions. Let them keep guessing. Nothing matters as long as I smile right and look beautiful. They did say I was the perfect height, and that I had the perfect Chinese eyes. It was in all the magazines. I saw it. I told uncle and auntie and my cousins that I was going to be a model one day, but they didn't believe me. They're stupid. I don't need to think about them anymore.

Once I get the money from this house, I'm going on a trip. It's about time I went somewhere outside of Singapore or Malaysia. Perhaps, I'll go to London. I've heard they like "Oriental" models in London.

It must be over two years now that I haven't seen my relatives in Kuala Lumpur. I haven't missed them, that's for sure.

You would have been proud of me, grandma. I did try hard not to let them see me cry. Sometimes, I thought that didn't make sense. Then, I'd be angry at you for ever making up the tree rule.

Now that I think about it, I do remember when I first felt the difference. You wouldn't have liked my cousins. They were nasty. Why did you make me leave Port Dickson and go to them in Kuala Lumpur?

Yes, I suppose you're right. I couldn't have stayed with you. I wanted to, you know.

But as I was saying, the time I guess I began to understand was when my aunt said my skin was too dark, and that dark skin was ugly on Chinese girls. That was the first thing. Then, my cousins began to tease me, and call me monkey. You know how the Chinese always call the Malays monkey? Well, that's what they called me.

Granny, how did you know I'd want to cry so much?

Did you know, once my cousins and I were playing during recess at school. It was right after I left you, so I must have been nine or ten. Right there, in the middle of the playground, they told everyone I was half person, half monkey, because I had a Malay mother. The other Chinese kids all started laughing. I stood there. I didn't know what to say. I used your tree rule for the first time since I left you. I closed my eyes, and tried to see the tree.

I saw it. The rough, patchy bark and spreading branches, those funny leaves, the rounded halves not quite matching. Then, I heard it, the soft whooshing sound of the buds blowing off the tree, the hard rain of the buds hitting the path.

The other children stopped laughing when they saw me standing there with my eyes closed. And they all went away.

After that, I got scared because my cousins went home and told their mother I was crazy. My aunt tried to get me to tell her what happened, but I refused because I knew the tree was none of her business.

I wouldn't have cared about their calling me monkey, except that they laughed at me. My girl cousin told me once I could never marry a Chinese because I was half monkey. When I said why not, my aunt said, don't you see, you stupid monkey, you're too ugly.

I was so furious I shouted at my aunt, and told her you

always said I was beautiful, just like my mother. My aunt said you were a crazy old woman.

What I don't understand about you, grandma, you're Chinese. So how come you think I'm beautiful?

It feels good to be off my feet, to be away from the spotlight and all the people telling me the same nonsense. How good you look! What a wonderful job you did! I wish I had a tan like yours! I know they say other things about me behind my back. Well, I don't need to worry about them. I've got it made.

Hadn't really thought about it, but I like not wearing make up and stupid designer dresses. They paint me like a doll, and dress me up, Then, they send me out on the catwalk, or trap me in their cameras. I feel naked in front of them.

Mmmm. This bed's comfortable. Nobody believed me, I don't think, when I said I had to come here to sell my house. It's fun to surprise people.

Everything's going to work out just fine. I'm only twenty, and I'm at the top of my profession with plenty of money. What could go wrong?

She was tiny, no more than four feet ten, I'd say. She used to say I shouldn't worry, shouldn't cry . . .

. . . oh you noticed, granny. Yes, I still wear it. You didn't mind, did you, that I took it away from the body? I knew you meant for me to have it.

I remember the first time you showed it to me. You said it was a tiny pendant for tiny people like us. I'm five feet seven now, granny, taller than you ever expected me to be.

You told me the three oval, pale green jade pieces were the buds from the raining tree. I believed you then. Yet, even after I knew better, I liked to think of those jade pieces as buds. You also said the gold setting was a gift from the tree ghost.

You meant the pendant for me.

They were only going to bury that pendant with her. Why shouldn't I have taken it?

I need to get some sleep. Tired.

Things move fast in Singapore. I like that. Don't have time to worry, or think about silly things. It's work all the time, seven days a week. Got to be efficient, professional. That's what the agency says. Funny city, Singapore. Even relaxing is fast. I never stop laughing, dancing, drinking. Someone gave me marijuana the other night. Those foreigners! They have everything. The English and Australian photographers keep telling me to get out of Asia. They say I'd do well in the West because I'm "exotic." Who knows?

Singapore's not like Kuala Lumpur. K.L.'s sleepy and old fashioned. Singaporeans are more exciting and worldly. Neil said so. he should know, because he's from London and has seen lots more of the world than I have. He said K.L. was a boring city in a boring country, and that if I knew what was good for me, I'd stay away from Malaysia. Makes sense to me.

Neil and the others laughed when I said I was going to Port Dickson. I don't care that it's not a big city here. It's country and quiet. Sometimes, I like quiet.

Half monkey, I mean, Malay. Is it the Chinese half they like? Neil said Malay girls were sexy, but slow.

I tried to run away from K.L. when I was thirteen. I'm twenty now, grandma. All grown up.

I was coming home to you. I had it all figured out. I'd get a bus to the station in town, and then walk out here. I didn't think it would be too far, because all the villagers walked. I remembered your telling me villagers never hurried or drove because they didn't want the rush to upset the ghosts. I always thought that was funny. When I was little, I kept imagining all the ghosts being knocked out of the way by our car.

Yes, I remember. You asked why I wanted the driver to stop that one time, and I said the rush of our car was upsetting the ghosts of Mummy and Daddy. You thought I was making that up, and that I was thinking about the accident.

You made up things all the time.

But let me finish. I had this big fight with Uncle and Auntie who wouldn't tell me you were dying. I told them they were letting you die. I even told them they hated me because of Dad, because he'd married a Malay. I knew they wanted the house, which was why they kept me away from you.

I know they thought I was defiant and stubborn, but they were never nice to me. My uncle thought it was funny to call me "monkey girl."

Granny, I'm not a monkey. There's nothing wrong with my being part Malay. Why did they have to think they were so superior?

Anyway, my uncle caught me trying to run away, and he said I deserved to be beaten. A beating would have been better than listening to him say our family was crazy. He called Dad an alcoholic, saying that's why he crashed the car. And then he called Mum no better than a whore, because she was cheap enough to be a model. He said Dad was craziest of all for marrying a monkey, and throwing away his money on this big house in Port Dickson.

I hated them, granny, I hated them. Most of all, I hated being monkey.

The Singaporean models are all mixed. They tell me I shouldn't even worry about marrying a Chinese. Anita says that. She's smart. She's a flight hostess for Singapore Airlines, and a part time model. I'd love to travel like her. Anita says I ought to marry a foreigner. Foreigners don't care if you're part monkey, I mean, Malay.

All the girls say Neil likes me. He does seem to. He told me I could easily get a job in London, and said he'd use his connections to help me.

Why do I have to think about all these things? I don't want to get married. Singapore's tiring. It doesn't make me feel beautiful anymore.

I'm sure Anita talks about me behind my back. Someone told me she used to sleep with Neil.

Why should I use Neil's connections? Maybe he's lying. Maybe he wants to make fun of me too. He probably wants to sleep with me, that's all.

Sometimes, I don't like Singapore.

They don't call me monkey now, granny. They wouldn't dare. You know something funny I heard? My girl cousin came to Singapore and tried to become a model! The agencies wouldn't even look at her. Auntie and Uncle were furious.

I wish you could come see me at the shows. Look, I brought you all the newspaper and magazine clippings so that you could see I'm not a monkey anymore.

She doesn't mind me coming home.

You know why I came back, don't you? I can't hide anything from you.

Do you think they're lying to me, granny? Everyone lies. They think it's the best way to control you.

Look at these clippings. They're making me something I'm not. That's no better than being a monkey girl all over again. Well, I won't do that, grandma. Why should I?

I'm tired of Singapore. I don't belong there.

Are you comfy, grandma? I want you to be as comfy as possible. I'll make some tea, and you can tell me a ghost story.

I'm tired of Singapore. I've had enough of modelling. It's silly pretending to be beautiful.

Grandma, I'm not a monkey.

It's evening now. I'm going to draw the curtains. I came home to rest, granny. Climb into bed with me, like you used to. Let's pretend, just for tonight, that we never left each other.

Look, granny, I can see our tree. Do you think it'll cry for me tonight?

THE SEA ISLANDS

If she looked real hard through the clouds she could see them. The sea islands. Misty, mysterious sea islands.

She knew all about them because once upon an aeroplane, her father had told her.

"See them? They're sea islands. Pieces of land under the sea that you can see from the sky. Mountaintops, plateaus that didn't quite make it to the surface when the world began. One of them could be the lost wolrd of Atlantis."

She had asked him then about this "Atlantis" and he told her about a once great civilization that just disappeared from the face of thc earth. How it sank. How the people had become mermaids and mermen who lived there now.

Ascent. The sea islands began to drift away from view. Now all she saw through the window were the cloud palaces. They were nice too, she decided, but not nearly as magnificent as the sea islands.

The tropical humidity that made her so uncomfortable was quickly forgotten in the air conditioned cabin of the aircraft. How grand she felt! Only eight years old and traveling all by herself. Well almost all by herself. It was a pity the airline insisted on a flight hostess escort. She looked at the woman in disdain. Rather stupid really. She hadn't even understood what she had meant when she told her about the sea islands. Anyway, she thought, something as important as sea islands should only be shared with important people, like her father,

It had been ten glorious sunny days with her father in Ko-ta-ki-na-ba-lu. She pronounced the name slowly to herself, noting every syllable the way her father had taught her to say it. That way, he had told her, she wouldn't forget how to spell it when she wrote letters to him. She took out of her bag the map her father had given her on which he had traced her flight path from East Malaysia to Hong Kong.

". . . right of the aircraft, you can see the peak of the famous Mount Kinabalu, which is 13,455 ft," the captain's voice announced over the intercom. Her eyes wandered back to her window. She gazed disinterestedly at the peak, and reverted her gaze for that final glimpse of her sea islands.

"If you could visit them," she remembered her father saying, "you wouldn't ever worry again, or cry, or be unhappy."

Was it a magic sort of place, she had wanted to know. Yes it was, according to her father. It was a sort of paradise.

In her mind she saw her tall, handsome American father. His skin was always brown from being out in the sunshine. It had been hot and sunny in Kota Kinabalu. She had sat on the beach and watched the tiny crabs making little sand castles out of sand balls all along the long sandy beach.

What were they doing those funny little crabs? She had pulled her Daddy-long-legs to the sand to see.

Too see the crabs!

What were they doing she demanded again, her determined Eurasian face staring at her father. Asking why why why. She had to know.

The crabs, she said. Why are the crabs making those little balls of sand and throwing them over their shoulders in sand-castle formations.

Her father smiled and picked up the balls of sand and gently laid them in his palm.

"The crabs are eating. They're taking all the small creatures out of the sand and leaving the hard, sandy particles in a ball."

Do crabs digest she wanted to know. Digest. It was a big word she had learnt for Dictation at school.

"Yes they digest. Just like you. Would you like to have crabs for dinner tonight?"

She nodded eagerly and ran down the beach to the water to play again in the warm ocean waves . . .

"Would you like a coloring book?" It was the air hostess standing by her seat interrupting the story in her mind.

No thank you she said. She had her own book to read. But if the hostess wanted to leave it she might get to it later.

Plane had stopped climbing now. Out of her window the distant setting sun tinted the clouds a soft pink hue. Like her nightgown. Her soft fluffy pink nightgown her mother had bought her.

She saw her mother's gentle dark eyes as if to scold, and the scolding change to tears. She had been confused. All she had asked her mother was couldn't she stay longer with her father in Kota Kinabalu and couldn't her mother come visit too.

"I have to stay in Hong Kong darling, otherwise, who would teach all my students while I was gone? Music exams are coming up soon, and my pupils need all the piano lessons they can get."

But if her mother came too Daddy would explain to all her students when he came home and then they wouldn't be angry at her. Her father could explain anything. She knew her father would come home soon after this business trip and all three of them could go visit Grandma in Connecticut at Christmas.

"Chasing dreams little girl. Like a butterfly." Her mother kissed her with a smile. "Goodnight." A lullaby sung in native Bahasa Indonesian to put her to sleep . . .

Opening the coloring book (childish, she thought, how like that stupid flight hostess to give it to her!), she wondered why her father had gone away for such a long time. Her father flew to lots of places in Asia. He was an engineer for a big American company. He was an important man, she knew, because he was so busy going places. It was so much fun the time he had taken her from their home in Hong Kong to Singapore. Her mother didn't go anywhere anymore. She didn't like flying! To her that was the silliest thing imaginable. She loved the huge aeroplanes, and the view of the land from the sky.

A voice on the intercom broke into her thoughts.

Something about dinner being served. She wasn't hungry. Anyway, it would be better to wait till she got home to have dinner with her Mommy. Her mother was a good cook. She made Indonesia food and Chinese food, and sometimes even big American steaks. And her mother was a beautiful lady. She loved to play with her long black hair, brushing and brushing it till it was shiny. Tying pigtails or ponytails or rolling it into a bun.

When she grew up she wanted to play the piano like her mother and travel all over the world like her father.

Her mother had promised to take her to Indonesia one day.

"You were born in Indonesia, you know. That's your home. When you were a little girl, your daddy and I took you everywhere. You've been to the States twice. Do you remember, the time you were four?"

Of course she remembered, she said importantly. That was in New Haven, Connecticut. And Granny knitted her a pink jacket because it was Christmas and cold. Now she could even spell Connecticut. And there was so much snow falling everywhere so pretty and white while Granny's dog braked and ran around in the snow. Could they go back again at Christmas she asked.

"I don't know. Maybe if your father stops chasing adventures and dreams, maybe . . ."

". . . over turbulence. Please keep your seat belts fastened."

She hadn't noticed but there seemed to be a storm outside. Oh good she thought. Maybe it was a typhoon. She loved curling up home in a typhoon. There would be no school that day, and her mother would play the piano for her and make something special for dinner.

The flight hostess came over and tried to fasten her safety belt.

She would do it herself thank you very much she said. These flight hostesses were such stupid women. Not like her mother. Her mother was clever, she had been to university. She'd bet none of these flight hostesses had ever been to university!

One day when she was grown up she'd go to university and study something difficult. Well maybe not too difficult. Just something difficult enough so that everyone would know she was clever.

What had her mother meant about chasing dreams and adventures she wondered sleepily. She hgged her teddy bear named Bear and tried to look out of the window.

It was dark outside and lightning was flashing across the skies.

What had her mother meant? Daddy-long-legs was always laughing and so happy. He made her laugh too. Like when he chased her and picked her up and tickled her to death. And she would laugh and laugh until she cried.

She had asked her father to make Mommy laugh too. She liked to see her mother laugh because she looked so pretty. That day on the beach, all three of them had run through the sea and laughed in excitement as the waves came crashing down.

Maybe if Daddy wouldn't go away so much Mommy wouldn't get so angry at him. Over their crab dinner in Kota Kinabalu she had asked her father to stay at home more often. Whe, she had wanted to know, did her father insist on making

Mommy cry so much by going away all the time. She knew he was an important man who had to go away on "business." But just what, what, what was this "business."

"I have to go. It's part of my job."

But why did he have to stay away so long, she demanded. Her father smiled at her.

"Well, I like the different places in Asia. They're well, they're so romantic I guess."

And what did "romantic" mean she wanted to know.

"It means something you love. You could say I'm in love with Asia."

She was puzzled. She thought, you see, that Daddy was in love with Mommy, wasn't he . . .

It was raining hard now. Outside it was pitch black. She had to go to the bathroom. The plane was so shaky.

A big hand helped to steady her. He was a tall man, like her father.

Coming back from the bathroom the flight hostess rushed her back to her seat.

Descent. The sea islands were coming back into view very quickly. She recognized the outline of Hong Kong below. She felt the flight hostess strapping her back into her seat. Why was this woman in such a hurry? In fact, she wondered, why was everyone in such a hurry?

Lights going out. Plane going down.

Good, she thought. We must be landing soon. She was excited about seeing her mother again. If only her mother wouldn't cry. Lately her mother cried so much. She had tried to tell her Mommy that Daddy would be home soon. Now she knew it was true because her father had promised her. She couldn't wait to tell her mother. He'd never break his promise to her.

A woman screamed. The sea islands were coming closer now. She could see the island of Hong Kong through the rain. So much noise and screaming. She wished it would all stop.

In the blur of descent she saw her father's face. He was swimming around a sea island with her mother. On the island Granny was sitting in her rocking chair and there was snow on the ground. The sun was shining so hot and bright on the sea and it was snowing in the sunshine of N-e-w- H-a-v-e-n, in C-o-n-n-e-c-t-i-c-u-t.

Last month she had written to Granny to thank her for the scarf she had sent her.

It was hot and cold, hot and cold. Sunshine and show and lots of sea and dogs barking.

She hugged Bear tighter. Her parents were swimming faster and faster now. They had tails like the mermaid and mermen in Atlantis that her father had told her about. Granny rocked harder and the snow in Connecticut fell more furiously. They were all telling her to jump, to jump onto that sea island and join them. Her sea island. That magic paradise.

Descent. The plane plummeted through the storm. Someone was making the sign of the cross.

She hugged Bear tighter and looked and looked harder at the sea island below. Jump. They were all telling her to jump. Her father, her mother, Granny in her rocking chair in new Haven, Connecticut.

Captain's voice on the intercom. Passengers screaming,

passengers crying. A big hand and arm reached out to her and hugged her. It was the tall man.

Mommy and Daddy and Granny are all waiting for me down there on the sea island can you see them — she was smiling smiling and so very happy.

There was her sea island in sight now. Mommy was laughing, Granny was smiling, and Daddy kept stretching his arm out for her.

Her father had kept his promise! She jumped.

FAMINE

I escape. I board Northwest 18 to New York, via Tokyo. The engine starts, there is no going back. Yesterday, I taught the last English class and left my job of thirty-two years. Five weeks earlier, *A-Ma* died of heartbreak, within days of my father's sudden death. He was ninety-five, she ninety. Unlike *A-Ba,* who saw the world by crewing on tankers, neither my mother nor I have ever left Hong Kong.

Their deaths rid me of responsibility at last, and I could forfeit my pension and that dreary existence. I am fifty-one and an only child, unmarried.

I never expected my parents to take so long to die.

§

This meal is luxurious, better than anything I imagined.

My colleagues who fly every summer complain of the

indignities of travel. Cardboard food, cramped seats, long lines, and these days, too much security nonsense, they say. They fly Cathay, our "national" carrier. This makes me laugh. We have never been a nation; "national" isn't our adjective. Semantics, they say, dismissive, just as they dismiss what I say of debt, that it is not an inevitable state, or that children exist to be taught, not spoilt. My colleagues live in overpriced, new, mortgaged flats and indulge 1 to 2.5 children. Most of my students are uneducable.

Back, though, to this in-flight meal. Smoked salmon and cold shrimp, endive salad, strawberries and melon to clean the palate. Then, steak with mushrooms, potatoes au gratin, a choice between a shiraz or cabernet sauvignon. Three cheeses, white chocolate mousse, coffee and port or a liqueur or brandy. Foods from the pages of a novel, perhaps.

My parents ate sparingly, long after we were no longer impoverished, and disdained "unhealthy" Western diets. *A-Ba* often said that the only thing he really discovered from travel was that the world was hungry, and that there would never be enough food for everyone. It was why, he said, he did not miss the travel when he retired.

I have no complaints of my travels so far.

My complaining colleagues do not fly business. This seat is an island of a bed, surrounded by air. I did not mean to fly in dignity, but having never traveled in summer, or at all, I didn't plan months ahead, long before flights filled up. I simply rang the airlines and booked Northwest, the first one that had a seat, only in business class.

Friends and former students, who do fly business when

their companies foot the bill, were horrified. You paid full fare? No one does! I have money, I replied, why shouldn't I? But you've given up your "rice bowl." Think of the future.

I hate rice, always have, even though I never left a single grain, because under my father's watchful glare, *A-Ma* inspected my bowl. Every meal, even after her eyes dimmed.

§

The Plaza Suite is 900 square feet, over three times the size of home. I had wanted the Vanderbilt or Ambassador and would have settled for the Louis XV, but they were all booked, by those more important than I, no doubt. Anyway, this will have to do. "Nothing unimportant" happens here at the Plaza is what their website literature claims.

The porter arrives, and wheels my bags in on a trolley.

My father bought our tiny flat in a village in Shatin with his disability settlement. When he was fifty and I, one, a falling crane crushed his left leg and groin, thus ending his sailing and procreating career. Shatin isn't very rural anymore, but our home has denied progress its due. We didn't get a phone till I was in my thirties.

I tip the porter five dollars and begin unpacking the leather luggage set. There is too much space for my things.

Right about now, you're probably wondering, along with my colleagues, former students and friends, what on earth does she think she's doing. It was what my parents shouted when I was twelve and went on my first hunger strike.

My parents were illiterate, both refugees from China's rural poverty. *A-Ma* fried tofu at Shatin market. Once *A-Ba* recovered from his accident, he worked there also as a cleaner, cursing his fate. They expected me to support them as soon as possible, which should have been after six years of primary school, the only compulsory education required by law in the sixties.

As you see, I clearly had no choice but to strike, since my exam results proved I was smart enough for secondary school. My father beat me, threatened to starve me. How dare I, when others were genuinely hungry, unlike me, the only child of a tofu seller who always ate. Did I want him and *A-Ma* to die of hunger just to send me to school? How dare I risk their longevity and old age?

But I was unpacking a Spanish leather suitcase when the past, that country bumpkin's territory, so rudely interrupted.

Veronica, whom I met years ago at university while taking a literature course, foisted this luggage on me. She's runs her family's garment enterprise and is married to a banker. Between them and their three children, they own four flats, three cars and at least a dozen sets of luggage. Veronica invites me out to dinner (she always pays) whenever she wants to complain about her family. Lately, we've dined often.

"Kids," she groaned over our rice porridge, two days before my trip. "My daughter won't use her brand new Loewe set because, she says, that's passé. All her friends at Stanford sling these canvas bags with one fat strap. Canvas, imagine. Not even leather."

"Ergonomics," I told her, annoyed at this bland and inexpensive meal. "It's all about weight and balance." And cost, I knew, because the young over spend to conform, just as Veronica eats rice porridge because she's overweight and no longer complains that I'm thin.

She continued. "You're welcome to take the set if you like."

"Don't worry yourself. I can use an old school bag."

"But that's barely a cabin bag! Surely not enough to travel with."

In the end, I let her nag me into taking this set which is more bag than clothing.

Veronica sounded worried when I left her that evening. "Are you sure you'll be okay?"

And would she worry, I wonder, if she could see me now, here, in this suite, this enormous space where one night's bill would have taken my parents years, no, decades, to earn and even for me, four years' pay, at least when I first started teaching in my rural enclave (though you're thinking, of course, quite correctly, well, what about inflation, the thing economists cite to dismiss these longings of an English teacher who has spent her life instructing those who care not a whit for our "official language," the one they never speak, at least not if they can choose, especially not now when there is, increasingly, a choice).

My unpacking is done; the past need not intrude. I draw a bath, as one does in English Literature, to wash away the heat and grime of both cities in summer. Why New York, Veronica asked, at the end of our last evening together. Because, I told her, it will be like nothing I've ever known. For the first time since we've known each other, Veronica actually seemed to envy me, although perhaps it was my imagination.

§

The phone rings and it's "Guest Relations" wishing to

welcome me and offer hospitality. The hotel must wonder, since I grace no social register. I ask for a table at Lutece tonight. Afterwards, I tip the concierge ten dollars for successfully making the reservation. As you can see, I am no longer an ignorant bumpkin, even though I never left the schools in the New Territories, our urban countryside now that no one farms anymore. Besides, Hong Kong magazines detail lives of the rich and richer so I've read of the famous restaurant and know about the greasy palms of New Yorkers.

I order tea and scones from Room Service. It will hold me till dinner at eight.

The first time I ever tasted tea and scones was at the home of my private student. To supplement income when I enrolled in Teacher Training, I tutored Form V students who needed to pass the School Certificate English exam. This was the compromise I agreed to with my parents before they would allow me to qualify as a teacher. Oh yes, there was a second hunger strike two years prior, before they would let me continue into Form 4. That time, I promised to keep working in the markets after school with *A-Ma,* which I did.

Actually, my learning English at all was a stroke of luck, since I was hardly at a "name school" of the elite. An American priest taught at my secondary school, so I heard a native speaker. He wasn't a very good teacher, but he paid attention to me because I was the only student who liked the subject. A little attention goes a long way.

Tea and scones! I am supposed to be eating, not dwelling on the ancient past. The opulence of the tray Room Service brings far surpasses what that pretentious woman served, mother of the hopeless boy, my first private student of many, who only passed his English exam because he cheated (he paid a friend to sit the exam for him), not that I'd ever tell since he's now a wealthy international businessman of some repute who can hire staff to communicate in English with the rest of the world, since he still cannot, at least not with any credibility. That scone ("from Cherikoff," she bragged) was cold and dry, hard as a rock.

Hot scones, oozing with butter. To ooze. I like the lasciviousness of that word, with its excess of vowels, the way an excess of wealth allows people to waste kindness on me, as my former student still does, every lunar new year, by sending a *laisee* envelope with a generous check which I deposit in my parent's bank account, the way I surrender all my earnings, as any filial and responsible unmarried child should.

I eat two scones oozing with butter and savor tea enriched by cream and sugar, here at this "greatest hotel in the world," to vanquish, once and for all, my parents' fear of death and opulence.

§

Eight does not come soon enough. In the taxi on the way to Lutece, I ponder the question of pork.

When we were poor but not impoverished, *A-Ma* once dared to make pork for dinner. It was meant to be a treat, to give me a taste of meat, because I complained that tofu was bland. *A-Ba* became a vegetarian after his accident and prohibited meat at home; eunuchs are angry people. She dared because he was not eating with us that night, a rare event in our family (I think some sailors he used to know invited him out).

I shat a tapeworm the next morning – almost ten inches long -- and she never cooked pork again.

I have since tasted properly cooked pork, naturally, since it's unavoidable in Chinese cuisine. In my twenties, I dined out with friends, despite my parents' objections. But friends marry and scatter; the truth is that there is no one but family in the end, so over time, I submitted to their way of being and seldom took meals away from home, meals my mother cooked virtually till the day she died.

I am distracted. The real question, of course, is whether or not I should order pork tonight.

I did not expect this trip to be fraught with pork!

At Lutece, I have the distinct impression that the two couples at the next table are talking about me. Perhaps they pity me. People often pitied me my life. Starved of affection, they whispered, although why they feel the need to whisper what everyone can hear I fail to understand. All I desired was greater gastronomic variety, but my parents couldn't bear the idea of my eating without them. I ate our plain diet and endured their perpetual skimping because they did eventually learn to leave me alone. That much filial propriety was reasonable payment. I just didn't expect them to stop complaining, to fear for what little fortune they had, because somewhere someone was less fortunate than they. That fear made them cling hard to life, forcing me to suffer their fortitude, their good health and their longevity.

I should walk over to those over-dressed people and tell them how things are, about famine, I mean, the way I tried to tell my students, the way my parents dinned it into me as long as they were alive.

Famine has no menu! The waiter waits as I take too long to study the menu. He does not seem patient, making him an oxymoron in his profession. My students would no more learn the oxymoron than they would learn about famine. *Daughter, did you lecture your charges today about famine? A-Ba* would ask every night before dinner. Yes, I learned to lie, giving him the answer he needed. This waiter could take a lesson in patience from me.

Finally, I look up at this man who twitches, and do not order pork. Very good, he says, as if I should be graded for my literacy in menus. He returns shortly with a bottle of the most expensive red available and now I know the people at the next table are staring. The minute he leaves, the taller of the two men from that table comes over.

"Excuse me, but I believe we met in March? At the U.S. Consulate cocktail in Hong Kong? You're Kwai-sin Ho, aren't you?" He extends his hand. "Peter Martin."

Insulted, it's my turn to stare at this total stranger. I look nothing like that simpering socialite who designs wildly fashionable hats that are all the rage in Asia. Hats! We don't have the weather for hats, especially not those things, which are good for neither warmth nor shelter from the sun.

Besides, what use are hats for the hungry?

I do not accept his hand. "I'm her twin sister," I lie. "Kwai-sin and I are estranged."

He looks like he's about to protest, but retreats. After that, they don't stare, although I am sure they discuss me now that

I've contributed new gossip for those who are nurtured by the crumbs of the rich and famous. But at least I can eat in peace.

It's my outfit, probably. Kwai-sin Ho is famous for her cheongsams, which is all she ever wears, the way I do. It was my idea. When we were girls together in school I said the only thing I'd ever wear when I grew up was the cheongsam, the shapely dress with side slits and a neck-strangling collar. She grimaced and said they weren't fashionable, that only spinster schoolteachers and prostitutes wore them, which, back in the sixties, wasn't exactly true but Kwai-sin was never too bright or imaginative.

That was long ago, before she became Kwai-sin in the cheongsam once these turned fashionable again, long before her father died and her mother became the mistress of a prominent businessman who whisked them into the stratosphere high above mine. For a little while, she remained my friend, but then we grew up, she married one of the shipping Ho's, and became the socialite who refused, albeit politely, to recognize me the one time we bumped into each other at some function in Hong Kong.

So now, vengeance is mine. I will not entertain the people who fawn over her and possess no powers of recognition.

§

Food is getting sidelined by memory. This is unacceptable. I cannot allow all these intrusions. I must get back to the food, which is, after all, the point of famine.

This is due to a lack of diligence, as *A-Ma* would say, this lazy meandering away from what's important, this succumbing to sloth. My mother was terrified of sloth, almost as much as she was terrified of my father.

She used to tell me an old legend about sloth.

There once was a man so lazy he wouldn't even lift food to his mouth. When he was young, his mother fed him, but as his mother aged, she couldn't. So he marries a woman who will feed him as his mother did. For a time, life is bliss.

Then one day, his wife must return to her village to visit her dying mother. "How will I eat?" he exclaims in fright. The wife conjures this plan. She bakes a gigantic cookie and hangs it on a string around his neck. All the lazy man must do is bend forward and eat. "Wonderful!" he says, and off she goes, promising to return.

On the first day, the man nibbles the edge of the cookie. Each day, he nibbles further. By the fourth day, he's eaten so far down there's no more cookie unless he turns it, which his wife expected he would since he could do this with his mouth.

However, the man's so lazy he lies down instead and waits for his wife's return. As the days pass, his stomach growls and begins to eat itself. Yet still the man won't turn the cookie. By the time his wife comes home, the lazy man has starved to death.

Memory causes such unaccountable digressions! There I was in Lutece, noticing that people pitied me. Pity made my father livid, which he took out on *A-Ma* and me. Anger was his one escape from timidity. He wanted no sympathy for either his dead limb or useless genitals.

Perhaps people find me odd rather than pitiful. I will describe my appearance and let you judge. I am thin but not emaciated and have strong teeth. This latter feature is most unusual for a Hong Kong person of my generation. Many years ago, a dentist courted me. He taught me well about oral hygiene, trained as he had been at an American university. Unfortunately, he was slightly rotund, which offended *A-Ba*. I think *A-Ma* wouldn't have minded the marriage, but she always sided with my father who believed it wise to marry one's own physical type (illiteracy did not prevent him from developing philosophies, as you've already witnessed). I was then in my mid-thirties. After the dentist, there were no other men and as a result, I never left home which is our custom for unmarried women and men, a loathsome custom but difficult to overthrow. We all must pick our battles and my acquiring English, which my parents naturally knew not a word, was a sufficiently drastic defiance to last a lifetime, or at least till they expired.

This dinner at Lutece has come and gone and you haven't tasted a thing. It's what happens when we converse over much and do not concentrate on the food. At home, we ate in the silence of A-Ba's rage.

What a shame, but never mind, I promise to share the bounty next time. This meal must have been good because the bill is in the thousands. I pay by traveler's checks because, not believing in debt, I own no credit cards.

§

Last night's dinner weighs badly, despite my excellent digestion, so I take a long walk late in the afternoon and end up in Chelsea. New York streets are dirtier than I imagined. Although I did not really expect pavements of gold, in my deepest fantasies, there did reign a glitter and sheen.

No one talks to me here.

The air is fetid with the day's leftover heat and odors. Under a humid, darkening sky, I almost trip over a body on the corner of twenty-fourth and seventh. It cannot be a corpse! Surely cadavers aren't left to rot in the streets.

A-Ma used to tell of a childhood occurrence in her village. An itinerant had stolen food from the local pig trough. The villagers caught him, beat him senseless, cut off his tongue and arms, and left him to bleed to death behind the rubbish heap. In the morning, my mother was at play, and while running, tripped over the body. She fell into a blood pool beside him. The corpse's eyes were open.

He surely didn't mean to steal, she always said in the telling, her eyes burning from the memory. Try to forget, my father would say. My parents specialized in memory. They both remained lucid and clear headed till they died.

But this body moves. It's a man awakening from sleep. He mumbles something. Startled, I move away. He is still speaking. I think he's saying he's hungry.

I escape. A taxi whisks me back to my hotel, where my table is reserved at the restaurant.

The ceiling at the Oak Room is roughly four times the height of an average basketball player. The ambience is not as seductive as promised by the Plaza's literature. The problem with reading the wrong kind of literature is that you are bound to be disappointed.

This is a man's restaurant, with a menu of many steaks. Hemingway and Fitzgerald used to eat here. Few of my students have heard of these two and none of them will have read a single book by either author.

As an English teacher, especially one who was not employed at a "name school" of the elite, I became increasingly marginal. Colleagues and friends converse in Cantonese, the only official language out of our three that people live as well as speak. The last time any student read an entire novel was well over twenty years ago. English Literature is not on anyone's exam roster anymore; to desire it in a Chinese colony is as irresponsible as it was of me to master it in our former British one.

Teaching English is little else than a linguistic requirement. Once, it was my passion and flight away from home. Now it is merely my entrée to this former men's club.

But I must order dinner and stop thinking about literature.

The entrees make my head spin, so I turn to the desserts. There is no gooseberry tart! Ever since *David Copperfield*, I have wanted to taste a gooseberry tart (or perhaps it was another book, I don't remember). I tell the boy with the water jug this.

He says. "The magician, madam?"

"The orphan," I reply.

He stands, open-mouthed, without pouring water. What is this imbecility of the young? They neither serve nor wait.

The waiter appears. "Can I help with the menu?"

"Why?" I snap. "It isn't heavy."

But what upsets me is the memory of my mother's story, which I'd long forgotten until this afternoon, just as I hoped to forget about the teaching of English Literature, about the uselessness of the life I prepared so hard for.

The waiter hovers. "Are you feeling okay?"

I look up at the sound of his voice and realize my hands are shaking. Calming myself, I say. "*Au jus.* The prime rib, please, and escargots to start," and on and on I go, ordering in the manner of a man who retreats to a segregated club, who indulges in oblivion because he can, who shuts out the stirrings of the groin and the heart.

§

I wake to a ringing phone. Housekeeping wants to know if they may clean. It's already past noon. This must be jet lag. I tell Housekeeping, later.

It's so comfortable here that I believe it is possible to forget.

I order brunch from room service. Five-star hotels in Hong Kong serve brunch buffets on weekends. The first time I went to one, Veronica paid. We were both students at university. She wasn't wealthy but her parents gave her spending money whereas my entire salary (I was already a working teacher by then) belonged to my parents. The array of food made my mouth water. Pace yourself, Veronica said. It's all you can eat. I wanted to try everything, but gluttony frightened me.

Meanwhile, *A-Ba's* voice. After four or more days without food, your stomach begins to eat itself, and his laugh, dry and caustic.

But I was choosing brunch.

Mimosa. Smoked salmon. Omelet with Swiss cheese and chives. And salad, the expensive kind that's imported back home, crisp Romaine in a Ceasar. Room Service asks what I'd like for dessert so I say chocolate ice cream sundae. Perhaps I'm more of a bumpkin than I care to admit. My colleagues, former students and friends would consider my choices boring, unsophisticated, lacking in culinary imagination. They're right I suppose, since everything I've eaten since coming to New York I could just as easily have obtained back home. They can't understand though. It's not what but how much. How opulent. The opulence is what counts to stop the cannibalism of internal organs.

Will that be all?

I am tempted to say, bring me an endless buffet, whatever your chef concocts, whatever your tongues' desire.

How long till my money runs out, my finite account, ending this sweet exile?

§

Guest Relations knocks, insistent. I have not let anyone in for three days. I open the door wide to show the manager that everything is fine, that their room is not wrecked, that I am not crazy even if I'm not on the social register. If you read the news, as I do, you know it's necessary to allay fears. So I do, because I do not wish to give the wrong impression. I am not a diva or an excessively famous person who trashes hotel rooms because she can.

I say, politely, that I've been a little unwell, nothing serious, and to please have Housekeeping stop in now. The "please" is significant; it shows I am not odd, that I am, in fact, cognizant of civilized language in English. The manager withdraws, relieved.

For dinner tonight, I decide on two dozen oysters, lobster and filet mignon. I select a champagne and the wines, one white and one red. Then, it occurs to me that since this is a suite, I can order enough food for a party so I tell Room Service that there will be a dozen guests for dinner, possibly more. Very good, he says, and asks how many extra bottles of champagne and wine to which I reply, as many as needed.

My students will be my guests. They more or less were visitors during those years I tried to teach. You mustn't think I was always disillusioned though I seem so now. To prove it to you I'll invite all my colleagues, the few friends I have, like Veronica, the dentist who courted me and his wife and two children, even Kwai-sin and my parents. I bear no grudges; I am not bitter towards them. What I'm uncertain of is whether or not they will come to my supper.

This room, this endless meal can save me. I feel it. I am vanquishing my fear of death and opulence.

There was a time we did not care about opulence and we dared to speak of death. You spoke of famine because everyone knew the stories from China were true. Now, even in this country, people more or less know. You could educate students about starvation in China or Africa or India because they knew it to be true, because they saw the hunger around them, among the beggars in our streets, and for some, even in their own homes. There was a time it was better not to have space, or things to put in that space, and to dream of having instead, because no one had much, except royalty and movie stars and they were meant to be fantasy — untouchable, unreal — somewhere in a dream of manna and celluloid.

But you can't speak of famine anymore. Anorexia's fashionable and desirably profitable on runways so students simply can't see the hunger. My colleagues and friends also can't, and refuse to speak of it, changing the subject to what they prefer to see. Even our journalists can't seem to see, preferring the reality they fashion rather than the reality that is. I get angry, but then, when I'm calm, I am simply baffled. Perhaps my parents, and friends and colleagues and memory are right, that I am too stubborn, perhaps even too slothful because instead of seeing reality, I've hidden in my parents' home, in my life as a teacher even though the years were dreary and long, when what I truly wanted, what I desired, was to embrace the opulence, forsake the hunger, but was too lazy to turn the cookie instead.

I mustn't be angry at them, by which I mean all the "them's" I know and don't know, the big impersonal "they." Like a good English teacher I tell my students, you must define the "they." Students are students and continue to make the same mistakes and all I can do is remind them that "they" are you and to please, please, try to remember because language is a root of life.

Most of the people can't be wrong all the time. Besides, whose fault is it if the dream came true? Post-dream is like post-modern; no one understands it but everyone condones its existence.

Furthermore, what you can't, or won't see, doesn't exist.

Comfort, like food, exists, surrounds me here.

§

Not wishing to let anger get the better of me, I eat. Like the Romans, I disgorge and continue. It takes hours to eat three lobsters and three steaks, plus consume five glasses of champagne and six of wine, yet still the food is not enough.

The guests arrive and more keep coming. Who would have thought all these people would show up, all these people I thought I left behind. Where do they come from? My students, colleagues, the dentist and his family, a horde of strangers. Even Kwai-sin and her silly hats, and do you know something, we do look a little alike so Peter Martin wasn't completely wrong. I changed my language to change my life but still the past throngs, bringing all these people and their Cantonese chatter. The food is not enough, the food is never enough.

Room Service obliges round the clock.

Veronica arrives and I feel a great relief, because the truth is, I no longer cared for her anymore when all we ate was rice porridge. It was mean spirited, I was ungrateful, forgetting that once she fed me my first buffet, teasing my appetite. Come out, travel, she urged over the years. It's not her fault I stayed at home, afraid to abandon my responsibility, traveling only in my mind.

Finally, my parents arrive. My father sits down first to the feast. His leg is whole and sperm gushes out from between his legs. It's not so bad here, he says, and gestures for my mother to join him. This is good. *A-Ma* will eat if *A-Ba* does, they're like that those two. My friends don't understand, not even Veronica. She repeats now what she often has said, that my parents are "controlling." Perhaps, I say, but that's unimportant. I'm only interested in not being responsible anymore.

The noise in the room is deafening. We can barely hear each other above the din. Cantonese is a noisy language, unlike

Mandarin or English, but it is alive. This suite that was too empty is stuffed with people, all needing to be fed.

I gaze at the platters of food, piled in this space with largesse. What does it matter if there are too many mouths to feed? A phone call is all it takes to get more food, and more. I am fifty-one and have waited too long to eat. They're right, they're all right. If I give in, if I let go, I will vanquish my fears. This is bliss, truly.

A-Ma smiles at the vast quantities of food. This pleases me because she so rarely smiles. She says, Not like lazy cookie man, hah?

Feeling benevolent, I smile at my parents. No, not like him, I say. Now, eat.

CITIZENSHIP

The bus from Buffalo jerked to a stop. Regina awoke abruptly, her head bumping against the window. How long had it been? A group of men boarded and headed towards the smoking section in back. One sat beside her.

Her book had fallen to her feet, and she bent to retrieve it, remembering.

Appeal denied.

That stamp across her F-1 student visa brooked such finality. Anger gave way to trepidation over the morning's futile mission. A stupid slip of paper stapled in her passport, and for that, the INS had made her wait two and a half hours.

Give up and leave, she told herself. Go back to Hong Kong. She had been warned of this outcome. Eight more days. The countdown to involuntary departure had shrunk from its original eleven, issued in Albany three days earlier.

"You from Buffalo?"

His voice startled her. Her seatmate leaned forward, hands jammed between his legs, smiling. He was Black.

Another pick up. It was time to stop being polite to this entire goddamned country. She refused to reply, refused to give in.

Two nights ago she had given in to the lure of sympathy at a bar in Albany. He was older, maybe even over thirty, with a voice like her Art professor's — husky, hopeful, never wrong — the man who lusted after her for two semesters. That afternoon, after waiting almost the entire day, an INS officer had returned her student visa with "cancelled" stamped across it and handed her a form letter which she read, uncomprehending.

"You're *deporting* me?" Her voice was soft. She did not look up at him.

"No, but you have to leave the country."

"But I've been accepted at grad school." She showed him her I-94 from the University of Utah. "What about that?"

He barely glanced at it. "If you leave by the deadline, nothing will go on your record. You'll just have to re-apply for a visa." He sounded embarrassed.

Her face was flushed. Tears fell. She wiped them away quickly, angrily. "But summer's almost over. You know it's too late. I'll miss fall semester. What if they don't hold my place for me?"

"You can appeal." His voice became faintly impatient.

"How?"

"You've got to go to Buffalo."

The ends of the earth! Did she even *know* anyone in Buffalo?

"Wouldn't be too hopeful, though," he added.

She wanted to shout — *you're ruining my life* — or argue in rational, persuasive tones, citing supporting evidence, the way she'd learned in Public Speaking. Instead, her voice turned desperate, pleading. "Can't I just cross over to Canada and re-enter? Please?" It was what Europeans did, she knew.

"You have to go back to your country of origin. Look, I don't write the rules. That's just the way it is." He walked away from the counter.

As she talked to the man at the bar who listened, anger failed her. She felt close to tears. Her voice became tremulous, timid, with that foreign squeak she despised. What use was her BA if she couldn't speak up and pass as American? Her English professors had advised — *go to grad school, find a specialty, get your PhD, teach* — they were probably right even if it wasn't what she really wanted. But she could get a J-1, perhaps even a green card and eventually, citizenship. That was the key to making things work, the way to fit into this country where life was big with prospects no matter what she did, as long as she worked the system. So when the Milton man said, *I was at Utah, I'll give you a good recommendation,* Regina said, sure, since Milton was as good a specialty as any.

The man bought her a drink. She kept talking, recasting her dreams, trying to sound like a winner not a victim, like a deserving foreigner who only broke the law to afford college.

Bad luck was all, she repeated, no one to blame. At the beginning of summer, the foreign student office was surprised at the sudden change in the law, when everyone's expected work visas were denied. *How did that happen,* he wanted to know, and she said what she'd been told, that President Nixon revoked the right foreign students had to work unconditionally during school breaks, the way she had legally worked in previous years. *So you're real mad at our president now?* No, she said, he did a good thing because he went to China. It was just his job to sign legislation.

She was drinking too fast, beginning to babble. Next she knew, he was saying, y'know, I have this friend in Buffalo, in city government — his hand rested across her arm — I could call, he might be able to help, adding, my place isn't far, as if that would make the difference, as if convenience somehow excused the lie. She threw her drink in his face and left. Vulnerability. It made her seem more naïve and foreign than she really was.

The man on the bus beside her said. "Hey, just talking. You don't want to talk, that's cool. I get off soon, anyhow." His voice was quiet.

Awlbany, the bartender at the club had said, as he poured her a free drink. *You gotta go to Awlbany and take care of it Regina. You gotta do things right.* He was from Brooklyn, a Poli Sci grad student at NYU, new on the job, and didn't know about her and Miguel, otherwise he might not have been so friendly. Miguel disappeared the minute Immigration showed up, leaving his manager to handle things. Miguel worked the system, and her. He was Colombian, and most days, Regina was in lust with him, wanting only attention and the advantage of being the boss' girl in return, both of which she got.

The two White officers barely noticed her at first, cornering instead all the dancers and waitresses who looked South American. Chang, the busboy, came out of the kitchen. He saw what was happening and ran. That was when one of the officers yelled, *grab the other one, she's one of them too,* and she felt his grip on her arm and knew it was all over. Yet Chang, that stupid Taiwan nerd, that four-eyed Computer Science creep, he'd escaped with his F-1 intact.

But the man next to her was just talking and there was no reason to be rude. Black faces usually asked less of her than White, that much she knew.

"Sorry." Her voice modulated off the foreign squeak. "Long trip."

"That's cool. You been visiting friends?"

Friends said it wasn't her fault. Earning money for college wasn't a crime, they said, better than stealing. No one could help, though, not really, except to tell her to go to Albany.

"No, visiting relatives," she lied. "In-laws. My husband and I live in Florida, but he had to work so he couldn't make this trip."

"Uh huh."

"He's a brother," she added.

"All right!" Her neighbor spread his enthusiasm to the others who echoed their appreciation. "What's he do?"

"He cooks, I waitress," and she wove an elaborate tale of

their summers in the Hamptons and winters in Fort Lauderdale. Chasing tourists, she said. Just like the people she met at Miguel's club in Manhattan, who worked here sometimes, there other times, even on board cruise ships, going wherever there was money to be made. A desirable life for a would-be poet and painter she felt, though not one her parents would approve. It was enough to live on and have adventures. If she could work, if she were a citizen.

Her seat mate was affable. A big guy, he shook as he laughed when she imitated the Lonnnggg Islanders, the snobs.

How easy to inhabit this fabrication. At least here, she could imagine a life. Four years away from home and "alien" *was* her state of being. If her parents only knew. Disbelief and shame. *To break the law, and for what, a job like that, running around half naked, serving men in a bar?* She never dared breathe a word about the art modeling, her legal on-campus job.

All they ever asked was why but not because they wanted answers. *Why poetry and painting? When you come home no one will employ you for studying arts.* Or why she hadn't returned with Rose at the beginning of summer. *But I can't say you haven't graduated,* her twin protested. *You went before me, they'll never believe it.* Luckily her sister kept secrets, and Regina stayed, pretending she was in summer school, saving every cent of her illegal earnings for grad school. Her professor assured, *don't worry, you'll get an assistantship after first semester,* apologizing that funds were scarce in English, especially for foreign students, unlike in Biochemistry or Computer Science.

"What's your name?"

"Suzie." The name tripped off her tongue. "Mrs. Suzie Washington."

"Pleased to meet you, Mrs. Suzie Washington."

"Likewise."

"You got any sisters?"

"One."

"She as pretty as you?"

To her surprise, she blushed, feeling thirteen again. He wasn't like the customers at the club, who gawked and pawed so predictably that sometimes she wanted to believe Miguel when he said things like, *all poetry or art is, is intellect pardoning lust.* Her seat mate was of an athletic build, with skin like polished rosewood. His features were handsomely proportioned. She suddenly wanted to draw him and opened her book to a blank page at the back. Her pencil rapidly sketched his likeness.

"What do you think?" She held out the page.

He held up both hands to receive it. "That's real good. Hey, look what she's done." He raised the book to show the men behind him. The chain of his handcuffs clinked against itself.

Regina glanced at his shackles. A uniformed man sat across the aisle.

He caught her glance and dropped his hands to his lap, still holding the book. His body seemed to shrink. "We get off soon," he said.

Should she be cautious, afraid? She didn't respond and didn't look at him.

"Down the ways," he continued. "Back inside, know what I mean?"

"Inside," she repeated. "What for?"

He leaned back and stretched his legs and arms. "Oh, this and that. Nothing serious. A little minor infraction, you know, like parking tickets. It's the all-American way." He laughed loud and long.

Subdued, Regina didn't know what to say. They traveled for awhile in silence.

In five hours or so, she'd be back in Albany, to transfer to the bus for New York. And then . . . here she came to a dead end. Was she to throw everything away just when life was beginning?

If only she hadn't gone to Albany!

She wasn't an illegal alien, and certainly not undesirable. The officer who picked her up more or less said so. *We were after the real illegals, you just happened in our way.* He didn't have any right to hold her, but procedure required he open a file and take away her visa. *And you've got to stop working, of course.* What about grad school, she asked, remaining cool as he eyed her body. *You'll have to go to Albany about that. Sweetheart, it's just the system.*

Worry creased her forehead.

Her seat mate interrupted her frown. "It ain't so bad Mrs. Washington. What's the matter? You got troubles?"

"A few."

"Don't worry too much. You'll get wrinkles." He offered a cigarette which she accepted.

They smoked. Her neighbor blew rings at the seat ahead, perfect circles.

"How long have you been inside?" Her question, self-consciously abrupt.

He shrugged. "Not long. Couple of years."

"That's rough."

"Not really. I don't think about it. It's easier."

His smoke rings bounced against the seat back, their circumferences dissolving into a vaporous mass. Four years ago, she had watched a tail of smoke disappear into the sky from the flight ahead of hers. Then, her plane rolled forward on the narrow runway towards the South China Sea, and she ascended into the air for the first time in her life, going away to America, away, she hoped, for good. Her mother's face, awash in tears, came into focus. *I can't bear for you to leave.* Regina had vanished behind the partition towards the immigration counters. The excitement, after years of impatient longing, of escape at last, overrode her family's sorrow. But at that moment of liftoff, as Hong Kong receded behind, she suddenly wept, unaccountably, uncontrollably. The student next to her offered a kleenex in sympathy, his own eyes already dried.

The bus swerved slightly round a curve. Her seatmate picked up the book, studied the cover and opened it. *Paradise Lost.* "Why you reading this hard stuff?"

"For coll . . . I mean, someone gave it to me. For the trip, you know."

"Sure. If you say so." His voice deepened in pitch. "We all need the hard stuff sometimes."

For a moment, she wanted to blurt out that everything was a lie, that she was scared, that all life was, was a trip from one fear to the next while pretending it wasn't. The officer in

Buffalo had been dismissive. He said it didn't matter where she left from as long as she left the country.

Fuck the INS they're less competent than you think, Miguel had said, the morning after the unexpected raid on his club. *This raid was a fluke. Someone tipped them off is all. They won't be back for a long time. Anyone can hide in New York, especially you, with hardly any accent. You just have to take your chances and be cool. Say you're my wife next time.* Miguel was the system as long as she needed to earn, because he gave her the best tables for tips and took care of her the way no one else could. *Forget the visa. You want to make money, you want to stay, right? So do it.* Miguel could be a bastard, but he was right about some things. *You're wasting your time with Albany,* he said, the night before she left, still hopeful.

The journey progressed. Regina dozed.

The bus halted in the middle of nowhere, waking her. There was no station. Across the field in the distance was a gray building. The Black contingent rose, all five of them, along with the two White officers whose guns were clearly in sight.

Her seat mate looked down. "Well, s'long, Mrs. Suzie Washington. That's what you call yourself, right?"

"That's right. See you."

"Not soon enough." He began walking down the aisle towards the door.

She called out after him. "Get out soon, okay?" The foreign squeak was gone.

Without turning round, he raised his hands above his head and waved a forefinger. "Tell your sister 'bout me."

Within minutes, the group was standing on the edge of the field, waving at her.

As long as she left . . . as long as she *didn't* leave and attempt to re-enter, no one would look for her. She could rip the cancelled visa from her passport, leaving the staple, leaving enough paper to identify it as an F-1 form, and claim her visa had been accidentally torn. If she went to another INS office, in Salt Lake City or L.A. perhaps, and showed the I-94 from Utah, they might never catch on. The foreign student office at her college upstate would confirm her original student status. They didn't know she'd worked illegally this summer and had gotten caught. INS didn't notify them because she had already graduated and was now in limbo. L.A., definitely. The INS there was bigger, more over worked, less likely to waste time on her.

In college, she wangled excuses for absence from classes, passed all her courses and was just smart enough for Milton. At the club, she was a terrific waitress, flashing smiles at customers, her long legs and midriff exposed, contributing to Sino-American titillation. She wouldn't have to rely on Miguel forever. She'd become legal somehow. Hope and a little luck was all she needed. She wasn't undesirable.

Her seat mate headed across the field. She waved at the others. As the group walked towards the gray building, she continued waving at their backs.

The bus jerked into motion. She looked around for her book, but it had disappeared. By the time she turned to see if he was holding it, the bus had already gone too far along the road.

RUBATO

I walk in dizzy on Good Friday. The club is half filled. Jazz blurts past me. Peggy and Ray, my San Franciscan Chinese-American friends, gave me my first hit of coke half an hour ago. We walk to our seats. The saxophonist blows a solo line. People clap.

Numbness suspends me. Jet lag lingers: my afternoon arrival from Hong Kong clings to my system. Peggy Lo smiles smoke rings at me. Ray Wong's fingers drum the table top: erroneous time to the rhythms of the quartet.

Peggy had said, half a year ago, "Come to San Francisco. I'll show you a good time. Introduce you to some real Chinese men. Ameri-Asian brothers."

Ray's fingers continue to drum. I count, his beats out of sync.

Peggy leans over and says, "Welcome to San Francisco."

I reply, "Do you know it's Good Friday?"

Ray looks at me. "Doesn't bother my Buddhist sensibilities," he says, smiling.

The music breaks, and Peggy and I go to the ladies' room. She tells me Ray wants to take me out. Privately, I refuse. Ray snorts coke every day.

This is my first trip to Peggy's city. Yesterday, I bargained with the curio dealer on Cat Street, and reduced the price of Peggy's gift by ten Hong Kong dollars. She would've been proud of me. Back in Hong Kong, where Peggy lived half a year ago, she called me her little sister-cousin, because she has two years on me. I am related to her in a distant, Chinese way, which means that four generations ago, her cousin married my grandaunt, or something like that. The difference was, her branch of the family immigrated to San Francisco, while mine found their way to Hong Kong. Now, as we leave the ladies' room, she tells me that Ray is generous with coke.

At our table, I look at Peggy, and remember her back in Hong Kong. Always fast and efficient. She strode, and I followed her, or wanted to, to the ends of the earth. In between the music, she tells me how glad she is to be back home. She loved the year in my city, and promises I'll enjoy grad school on the East Coast after my seven year absence from the U.S. I look at Ray. He is still smiling at me. How is it Peggy knows Ray wants to take me out? Perhaps because he does look at me.

The music rises in volume. I feel the numbness give way to an edgy dissonance. Peggy chain smokes, talking non-stop.

When she does stop to take a long drag, Ray cracks a bad joke about the Resurrection. I watch his glazed eyes, tinged with coke. I want to tell him, with an as inscrutably straight face as I can muster, that I'm a devout Catholic.

The piano player glides into a lingering solo. I watch, impressed, as Ray fingers a transcription on the table top.

Peggy says, "You should hear Ray play. He's good."

Ray hides his hands in his lap. "Come off it, Peg. You know better than that."

Peggy doesn't give up. She winks at me, tells him, "Why don't you play for us tonight?" Then, indicating me, "She plays too. Chopin."

Ray looks at me, suddenly interested. The glaze in his eyes disappears. "Okay," he says, "let's go to my place."

Now it's my turn to be embarrassed. I remember telling Peggy back in Hong Kong that I seldom dated Chinese men because they found me too Westernized, and wanted to get serious too quickly. It's easier for me, as a travel writer in Asia, to casually date foreign men I meet outside of Hong Kong. Ray, according to Peggy, usually dates Jews and WASPs, and wants to meet a Chinese woman who isn't looking to get serious.

We get up and leave. Peggy grins. There's nothing inscrutable about her expression. "Do I leave early?" she whispers to me.

I am suddenly happy, and want to laugh.

Outside, we wait while Ray gets his car. San Francisco in April is cold. I shiver; my body recalls the heat of the sun over the South China Sea. This is not the America I remember, where Chinese persons can behave American with impunity, which *doesn't* only mean drugs, cigarettes, booze, sex, jazz clubs or anything else "the elders" mean. Seven years back home after college took America out of me, except when I traveled abroad. And then, Peggy Lo came into my life and said, come back to America.

Ray's Honda pulls up. We climb in; I make sure I grab the back seat on the excuse that I'm smaller. Ray turns around.

"Comfortable?"

I nod.

We arrive fifteen minutes later. Inside Ray's Duncan Street two bedroom apartment, the place is half empty. I look around, curious.

"My elder brother moves in next week for three months," he explains. "You know, Confucian family ties."

I know what he means. When I left Hong Kong, I gave my flat and all my furniture to my sister.

The upright is in a corner by the window. Ray opens it, and pulls up a stool. Peggy flops on a cushion in the opposite corner.

"So play." He offers me the piano stool.

I sit. Jet lag doesn't relent. I play the opening of an Easter hymn.

"Peg!" Ray's voice, embarrassed. "Why didn't you say she was Christian?"

"Serves you right for cracking religious jokes," she retorts, unsympathetic.

I laugh. "I'm a lapsed Catholic," I say, reassuringly. "Converted to Buddhism."

Now it's their turn to laugh.

"Yeah, sure," he says, "and I'm a Kung Fu master."

"Come on," Peggy drawls from her corner, "play."

I comply with Chopin's fourth prelude, my fingers on automatic. I memorized the piece as a child in Hong Kong. My childhood piano teacher's Austro-Germanic accent growls in my ear. *Why do you play it Rubato?* My left hand regulates the chords, trying for an even rhythm. Trying to respect the time that it's written in, instead of molding the melody with the robbed time of a Rubato. Always trying. For what? Relax, I tell myself. No great expectations here. You made it back to America, to Peggy's promised Asia America. Where you can say you're Buddhist because you don't expect to fool anyone.

The prelude rises and falls. I've always been just an okay player, nothing more, even after twelve years of lessons. My parents believed in over-education, to prepare their precious offspring for college in America. Piano lessons, ballet lessons, French classes as well as twelve years of American nuns, British educators, and Chinese teachers in Hong Kong coaching me in the English-American language, Western culture, history and civilization, and establishing a strong grounding in the Sciences and Advanced Mathematics, while insisting I continue a study of Chinese language, literature, history and culture. *Too much Rubato, you play too much Rubato.* And finally, college. Being one of five Chinese students at a tiny, Catholic, New England campus that my parents picked out for me. Independent and alone at seventeen. Readied to face America. Who was I supposed to be? What was I supposed to think and do? Who was I to date? They were furious when I told them I had a militant Black boyfriend.

Peggy and Ray listen to me play. Their parents believed in the same things too, and they already were in America. Ray's a computer programmer and an architect, who plays piano and violin. Peggy's a lawyer, and a civil rights advocate in San Francisco's Chinatown. She left a six figure corporate law job at the age of twenty nine to spend a year in Hong Kong improving her Cantonese. And she paints. She's the only Chinese artist I know who can't paint bamboo. But she's trying.

My fingers slow down to the final chord. It is not marked Rubato. I am grateful they receive the ending in silence.

Ray's turn. He plays something by Rachmaninoff. I am surprised by his control, by the power in his hands. Most of all, I am surprised by the firm rhythm. Maybe I imagined his erroneous time, earlier at the club.

He ends the piece prematurely, and launches into the Moonlight. I whisper to Peggy, "He plays much better than me."

She nods in agreement; her eyes smile. I wonder if Peggy isn't in love with Ray.

Jet lag begins to dissolve. The irritable edge I feel from the coke gives way to a pleasant tingling. My eyes wander to a photograph on the bookshelf. Ray and another Chinese man. The Chinese characters for "elder brother" are scribbled in the corner. He is sexier than Ray, who looks like a Chinese version of the Marlboro man. The brother is slighter in build, more untidy. More Chinese.

I bum a cigarette from Peggy. She lights it for me. Ray

finishes playing and comes to join us.

"Nail in your coffin, too," he says to me. "What is it with you Hong Kong women?"

We laugh. Ray is definitely not my type.

We head to the Top of the Mark, which, says Peggy, is the best vantage point for San Francisco by night. Back home, I took Peggy to the top of the Sheraton in Kowloon one night to show her the lights of the "fragrant harbor," which is what Hong Kong means. That night, she told me we both shared a future duty, a trip to the mainland of China, something neither of us had yet done. She also said that she would never have to live again as Chinese as she had in Hong Kong, that her next Chinese search was bound to be easier. I wanted to hug her, to thank her for talking about what I felt but could not say.

But I didn't. Chinese in Hong Kong don't hug, especially in public places.

At the top of the Mark, Peggy and Ray stand by the plate glass window and pick out landmarks. I am a little behind them. They look good together. Peg and Ray. Tall Chinese. She is at least five foot eight, and Ray is almost six foot. Peggy places her hand on his arm, and gestures excitedly at something. Ray has one hand in his pants pocket. Very casual. At five foot three, an average Hong Kong woman height, I feel small.

Ray stretches out his arm, places a hand on my shoulder, and draws me between them.

"Peggy says you write."

"I try to."

"What do you write about?"

"People. Places. Being Chinese in a Western World."

"Is it always a Western World?"

Peggy interrupts. "Let's get a drink, guys."

The tables are filled, and we sit at the bar which snakes like a river. Ray sits between us, at a protruding curve. His eyes are clear.

Our drinks arrive.

Ray lifts his glass. "So let's drink to Good Friday."

Peggy clinks her glass against mine. "Forget Good Friday. Welcome back to America."

"Will I really be happy in New England?" I ask.

"Of course," Peggy smiles, adding, "you're only twenty eight. That's not too old to go back to school, or to start writing what you really want to. It's different now. You're not seventeen anymore. This is America, not Hong Kong. We beat you to the colonial overthrow, remember?"

She's right, I think. And suddenly I feel I need never go back to Hong Kong again, that I've left it behind me in favor of being Chinese in the real Western World, in the culture which is as much my own as my Chinese heritage. Perhaps, I should have opted for grad school on the West coast, where there is an Asia-America. I am afraid of the isolation ahead. Will New England still have the romance that engulfed me as a starry eyed English undergraduate? Or will I just be marking time, while burying ghosts?

A voice from behind startles me.

"Excuse me, but did you say you were going to New

England?"

The Caucasian man sitting next to me is a New Englander from Boston. He chats with me for a few minutes. Bar chat. I know if I were alone, he would try to pick me up. He carries on about his recent visit to Hong Kong, about 1997, proud that he knows about China's impending "takeover," as he calls it, about Chinese food. Ray smiles, and puts his hand over mine on my barstool. Peggy lights yet another cigarette, and blows smoke rings into the lights above the bar. Our New Englander enthuses on. He *loves* sweet and sour.

Ray announces. "It's midnight. Good Friday's over."

The three of us laugh, freezing out our New Englander. He turns away and starts chatting up two women on his right.

Peggy sees some people she knows and excuses herself to speak to them.

I sip my scotch. Ray's hand is still on top of mine. Peggy returns with three Chinese-Americans, two men and a woman, all of whom Ray appears to know. We move to a table.

We talk, and laugh. Peggy tells everyone at the table that she is trying to get me to stay through the summer. I smile, knowing I'll leave in three days.

Before I sleep tonight, I think I will hear that Austro-Germanic accent again. My piano teacher hit my hand with a ruler once, because I did not play a piece at just the right tempo. I had held back my tears, and carried on playing.

I'm still playing. I'm back in America.

PINEAPPLE UPSIDE DOWN BIRD

A young Chinese woman stood, overlooking Trafalgar Square, and waited. Wintry day. Killing time in a foreign city. Waiting: having arrived two hours too early for an appointment with friends. Looking and overlooking. Simply that. Not anticipating, not expecting. Stepping backwards, away from the stone railing.

A bird fell. It brushed past her shoulder and landed behind her. Upside down. Startled, she turned around. A photographer's flash: a moment and over. She and the photographer stooped over the bird, contemplating its upside-down state.

That was how they met. She, killing time and bumping into falling birds. He, killing time, cruising London's streets with the ever observant eye of The Photographer. He was Anthony

Dewar, from Edinburgh.

Did they "have coffee" to ponder the bird's fate? Did they smile and fall in love? Did they eventually exchange, in some third-class hotel room, the stories of their lives, of their arrival in this foreign city?

No.

He apologized. For startling her with his flash. For attempting to capture her comic look of bewilderment at the sight of the bird, upside down.

She cradled her palm underneath the bird's back, and turned it right side up. The bird stood up, and flew away.

"It must have got tired while flying," he said.

"Stupid bird," she said.

They did not stop there. Killing time together they went to a photo exhibition. Faces. From all over the world. The exhibited photographer, a woman, had gathered faces for a London public's consideration.

"I think she's good," he said. "I would like to travel like her, like you. To Europe, Asia, the Middle East, America. Gathering remembrances."

Her home in Southeast Asia held more remembrances for her than all the foreign countries she had seen, she said. The photographer of the exhibit could have found those racially diverse faces right here in London. "Don't you think so?" she asked.

Anthony Dewar smiled and said he did not know. He had never left the United Kingdom. This was his first trip to London.

Sometimes, she remembers that moment. Could she have

taken him with her then in spirit? When they exchanged addresses — his in Edinburgh, hers in new York (her home-to-be in nine months) — she knew that they would never meet again unless she went to Edinburgh. Oh she *could* go to Edinburgh. But she did not *need* to go to Edinburgh, anymore than she needed to go to any corner of the world.

They parted at the top of Trafalgar Square. It was three o'clock. When she met her friends for tea that afternoon, she ordered a pineapple upside-down cake. "Just like in the bakery back home!" she explained. "Are there pineapple upside-down cakes in Hong Kong bakeries?" her London friends asked, surprised. "No," she replied, "just in the one opposite our home when I was a child. The baker's wife was English, permanently expatriated in Hong Kong with her Chinese husband. She had a mildly cockney accent."

She left London a week later. Anthony Dewar, she presumed, had returned to his home in Edinburgh. Travel kept her busy in Europe: museums, cheap and beautiful Southern isles, bread and wine. People! All over Europe there were people she wanted to meet and people who wanted to meet her. It was comical, this indulgence in people. "Let us go to Italy," said one traveler friend. "Shall we meet in Paris? London? Frankfurt?" "What about a little Greek island hopping?" "Take me to Asia." Multitudes of people, making enthusiastic promises that would be ridiculous to keep.

In a little notebook, she wrote down character sketches of many of the people. Sometimes, she also wrote descriptions of blues seas, white rocks, city squares. When she was no longer moved by people and places, she jotted down remembrances of the Hong Kong she could not longer live in. "There is no room for an artist in Hong Kong," she wrote, as she contemplated Ivan the Terrible's architectural contribution to Red Square ("A fairy-tale picture book building.") Years later, on the subway in new York, she read in Miller's *Air Conditioned Nightmare*, "there is no room for an artist in America," and thought that possibly, just possibly, Miller was as wrong as she had been.

But most of the time, during her sojourn in Europe, she wrote down impressions of people. Neatly. In her little notebook. What mattered, after all, except the people she laughed with, danced with, cried with, learned with, loved with? Was this not life?

Four months after the Trafalgar Square day, she sat down to dinner in her married sister's Paris apartment.

"And for dessert," declared her sister, the family's culinary queen, "pineapple upside-down cake! How's that?'

Of course she loved it. They giggled together over remembrances – from long before her sister had met and married the Middle Eastern Frenchman studying engineering in an American university. He ignored their sisterly plunges into a past he did not share.

"What a silly fuss over a cake," she said.

"All because the baker's wife wore low-cut sweaters and her tits practically hung out," said her sister. "No one, we thought, could have tits that big or skin that white. Like an English cow's milk."

Her sister said the last phrase in Chinese, at which point she erupted in laughter.

"But even then we knew perfectly well that the Chinese have cows too," she objected, cutting through the illogic of her sister's remembrance.

"Yes, and Chinese women have excuses for tits, and steamed cakes, and art and literature and cities and universities . . ."

"But they don't have pineapple upside-down cake," she finished.

Sitting in her sister's Paris apartment, she wondered whether travels added to remembrance or clouded her vision. She began to tell her sister about London, the bird, Anthony Dewar.

"So are you going to Edinburgh?" her sister asked at the end of her narrative.

"What for?"

"Why for him, of course."

"You must take me for an incurable romantic! Didn't you say I collected more people than I needed?"

"But what other reason would you have for traveling so much?"

"To record people, places, things. For my novels."

"Rubbish. You can do that in your flat in Hong Kong. The only reason you go after greener grass, as you do, is because grass was never green to you in the first place. I'm just surprised you never get tired."

Sitting in her sister's Paris apartment, she ate the freshly made pineapple upside-down cake. It was delicious. It truly brought back memories of a Hong Kong girlhood waiting to reach the source of a pineapple upside-down cake. Perhaps the anticipation, the wait, was the source itself. Perhaps now, contrary to her sister's belief, she was experiencing the tiniest tinge of fatigue.

She went to Edinburgh, of course. Just as she went to Moscow, Paris, Chicago, Singapore. Just because it was a place once presented to her in a context she could not forget.

So she went to Edinburgh. Because a bird in London once almost fell on her head. Because she was at loose ends between the fifteenth and twentieth of May that year. Because her secondary school math teacher had been a Scottish grand dame who had taught her young Hong Kong charges the correct curtsey to affect before Queen E. Because she had once loved a Scotsman.

It was a memorable city. There were crumbling pillars on a hilltop that excited her imagination. There was the cleanest and cheapest B&B of her travels. There was, coincidentally, a gathering of the clans which produced a fanfare of kilts and bagpipes. Could there have been a more cooperative city for the traveler?

No.

Even Anthony Dewar was free for a day to accompany her round the sights and to his local pub.

Was he enthralled by the sudden-ness of her visit? Did they wander to some romantic spot, as adventurers are wont to do, and discover the force that drew them together in the frist place? Did they, after several bitters and a hearty Scottish meal, repair to his studio and make mad, passionate love in the dark room? Did he, moved by the fact that he had never met a Chinese woman before, photograph her as an eternal memory?

No.

Anthony Dewar said, "The shot of you in London came out badly, I'm afraid. So I junked it."

"I've always been unphotogenic," she apologized.

They walked around a graveyard, and talked about T.S. Eliot. This was what they shared: a love of Eliot's poetry. Hers had begun on a hot and humid autumn's day in an un-air-conditioned classroom where an Indian teacher, complete with sari, had declaimed lines from "Rhapsody on a Windy Night," and subsequently entered the class in a speech contest where Chinese schoolgirls performed a choral recitation of the poem by the American who transferred his allegiance to England. And from there her acquaintance with the poet mushroomed into love. Anthony Dewar made her remember, forced her to recall a Hong Kong girlhood she was rapidly leaving behind.

Then he spoke of himself as an Edinburgh man, complete with kilt. London had proved a disappointment. Now, he said, he wanted to go to New York. Photography was born in America, after all.

He left her that day with a gift: a volume of the Four Quartets. No inscription.

At the end of her European sojourn she repaired to America with an address book full of European names. Within a year, most of the names had become words on a page. The people lived only in her character sketches. Sometime in that year she had read about an ambassadress in a James' novel who "collected" people. Now, flipping through her address book, she understood her Paris sister's passion for philately.

Except for one thing.

The Anthony Dewars of the world defied collection. To obtain the rarest postage stamps required only patience, money, and the art of seducing postage stamps.

He never wrote, never came to New York. A horde of others came instead to entertain her. It amazed her that people wanted to be collected, practically begged to be collected, at least for short periods of time. Occasionally, there was famine of collectibles, but that always quickly passed because a new collectible would eventually appear.

In one of her sister's letters: "How is it you meet so many people? I go to work, live life, and hardly ever meet a soul. Yet, you. Birds fall on your head in the middle of Trafalgar Square and you meet an interesting person. It doesn't seem as if you even try very hard. Your life is too full of coincidences. Don't you ever get tired?"

Yes, she thought, sitting in her comfortable but empty apartment, she did.

One day, she rolled a blank index card into her typewriter and wrote: "Pineapple Upside-down Bird." The words had a nice feel to them. She stared out of the window for several minutes. Then she went to the kitchen and brewed a pot of Japanese tea. It looked too green.

She sat down at her typewriter and tried, again.

"The story of A.D."

A sip. Ouch. The tea burnt her tongue.

"One day in Trafalgar Square, a bird falls on her head."

She looked at the card, ripped it out of her typewriter, and stuck it into her "yes-maybe-never" ideas file. In the corner of the card she marked an "n."

Time passed.

Visiting a college campus in Western Massachusetts. Killing time wandering around a concrete square avoiding the Walkmanned roller-skaters. Under a leaning metal arch – modern sculpture – waiting for a bus back to New York with an hour to spare. Moving away from the square. Passing a gallery. Going in.

There was a photography exhibition of people-less places. From all over America. She peered at rolling waves and undulating sand dunes. Soft, round shapes. Fluid shapes. People-less nature in motion. Musical. The photographer was a man of whom she hadn't heard.

A bus to New York with ten minutes to spare.

By the bus stop at the square, a single note wailed into the air. All the waiters-for-the-bus turned to look at the student practicing bagpipes across the square. The single note broke into a cascade of sound. Wails. "Scotland the Brave."

She remembers suddenly that on the day she left Anthony Dewar in Edinburgh he kissed her goodbye. An airy brush across her lips. Ethereal yet sensual.

A small audience collected around the bagpiper.

The bus to New York arrived. She boarded. The bus pulled away. Last chorus of "Scotland the Brave."

OUR BODIES REMEMBER

THE ART OF LOVE

They say time stops for no man, that time marches on, commonplaces that are still repeated, yet there are people who chafe at the slowness with which it passes. Twenty four hours to make a day, and at the end of the day you discover that it was not worthwhile, and the following day is the same all over again, if only we could leap over all the futile weeks in order to live one hour of fulfillment, one moment of splendor, if splendor can last that long.

from *The Year of the Death of Ricardo Reis*
José Saramago (1984)
Translation by Giovanni Pontiero (1991)

Their last night together was spent on a beach. Sonny was not to see Victoria again for eighteen years until November of '99, the year his work was honored by the Academy of American Poets.

She was in the audience the evening he read from his latest volume at the University of Hong Kong, in English and Chinese, as the press took pains to note the next morning. Sonny Pessoa performed, pretending not to see her. Afterwards, Victoria Chang-Howell waited till the crowds had thinned.

"I thought it was you." He air-kissed both cheeks, with just enough distance for fame.

"You look the same," she said. At fifty seven, she passed for younger. Her hair was coal black, dyed to match her eyes;

crows' feet, however, were harder to hide. She had dressed for
the occasion, uncharacteristically sensual, imitating an earlier
self. At fifty seven, she felt their age difference, the way she
hadn't, eighteen years earlier.

"And you're," he took in her expensive appearance —
quirky, almost artistic, but less effective than he remembered
— annoyed because, yes, she still provoked desire. "You're
marvelous to see again. What are you doing with yourself
these days? Are you still at the ad agency?" His sentences
weren't even poetic.

"I left big agency life ages ago." She rarely thought of those
days, Sonny being the vestigial exception. "We have our own
creative boutique now, and handle mainly luxury and travel
accounts. We keep a home in Bali." Realizing he might not
know, she added, "by the way, I did marry . . ."

"Howell?" He said it for her.

Eighteen years ago, Bruce Howell had been the highest-paid
advertising "creative" in town and a painter — British,
divorced, childless, older, a worthy partner for Victoria —
against whom Sonny, a third-rate copywriter and unknown
poet paled, despite his richer tan.

Then he did know, she thought, miffed. Sonny had been
the jealous type. Surely, some spark remained. "And yourself?
Are you married?"

"Was. Split up over two years ago." If he could he would
have held back time, but the moment for amends was already
past.

"I'm sorry to hear that." Yet she was strangely pleased.

"Don't be. I wasn't the faithful type." It felt like an

accusation — *unintentional* — as was his confession — *glib*, a pose to impress — but despite her half smile — *suggestive* — he tried to move on and asked. "And you. Do you still paint?"

But she was handing him her card, saying, "I mustn't hold you up," even though no one was displaying any urgency and it wasn't late. "We must see each other while you're here. Have you a card?"

"I don't carry any," he replied, but obliged by dictating his number, giving her, as their history demanded, the perpetual upper hand, with which she touched his, before departing.

§

On that beach, sand pebbles chafed. Sonny had been twenty four. Victoria liked being on top, exposing her breasts to the night.

It was just spring, too cold for the flocks of summer. Besides, no one will be around she insisted, frustrated by two months of furtive trysts, unsatisfactorily consummated in the back seat of her car. Victoria was in between husbands; with her first marriage not quite over and her relationship with Bruce Howell indeterminate, she had need of, if rarely a bed for, an easier love. Discretion was all she asked.

But that night he gave more, far greater than her imagination could begin to absorb. His heart succumbed to the song of the tide, indulging the art of love.

§

In the morning, he flung aside the *South China Morning Post* in disgust.

Their coverage of his reading included the following. "His latest volume, *Love's Exile,* is a *cri de coeur* of the emigrant, who leaves but never arrives, tracing song-lines for trans-national lives. Pessoa exhibits only a grudging respect for his origins, the result, no doubt, of an American life. The poet, whose father is the linguist Dr. Antonio Pessoa, is by now only marginally a 'native son,' despite his return to our shores. Nonetheless, his affair with the language tantalizes, even as it irritates."

The local English journalist concluded on this note. "Sonny Pessoa has proven almost his father's equal as a translator."

He wanted to shriek. Could he *help* his love of the English language?

From eighteen years earlier, his father's voice carped. *You should be ashamed of your betrayals,* meaning his abandonment of Chinese and Portuguese. His Macanese parents were both Eurasian. After his mother's death, Sonny had been removed from Macau at age four to Hong Kong, where English surpassed both mother tongues.

Coming home now — surely Hong Kong was still home, this city that bestowed "permanent" residency, at least on his identity card — he came armed with a bilingual volume of poems which included his own translations into Chinese, but not Portuguese.

The Chinese press, unlike their English language counterpart, were surprisingly unstinting in their praise. Lavish, almost fulsome, because his poetry paid homage to China but not Britain. Sonny savored it, comforted, even as he worried if this could sustain.

He did not call Victoria.

Homecoming stirred regrets. Vague, even pointless, they

lingered. At night, waves pounded through his dreams, and he awoke, drenched in memories, afraid.

When she rang two days later because he hadn't, she accused in Chinese. "You promised you'd stay in touch. I wondered where you were. I don't follow Poetry, I'm afraid, but would have replied had you written."

Could it be that she'd never received his letter? *Love plays memory for a fool,* it read. *Work honors me — I have won an important American poetry prize and been granted a fellowship to work on Chinese translations.* Had her silence, then, been ignorance and not rejection? Now, remembrance, with its bad habit of arriving always too late (sometimes, inconsequentially so), stirred the muddy hole and fished out Victoria's precise instructions of eighteen years earlier. *I don't have a forwarding address yet but Penny Wong, my assistant, will know where I've gone, she's not the moving type,* because Victoria had also been in between jobs. He hadn't dared ask Penny, though, not since fucking her after a party — he promised but never called, to the profound chagrin of young Penny, ignorant of being the rebound. His letter, when it arrived on her desk from New York, was not forwarded. Penny had not initially connected him with Victoria, the troublesome.

Victoria was still speaking. "What brings you back?"

"This and that. The handover." Her familiar phone manner was disconcerting, recalling their long ago trysts. His hand grazed his son's photo, which sat beside the phone.

"Aren't you a little late?"

"Not for Macau."

But she was back on that beach, and unconcerned by the

politics of his birthplace. The return to China she cared about had already passed. "I thought you were here for your father." That Dr. Antonio Pessoa was to be honored next week by the Law Society (for his precise and useful translation of a significant body of local legalese into Chinese — imperative since the British no longer prevailed) did *not* escape her notice. Victoria's father, Sir Albert Chang, OBE, deceased, had been a prominent solicitor and she followed Law.

He bristled. "That, too."

"You must be proud of him." It was not what she meant to say but Bruce was within earshot, having returned unexpectedly. Her husband knew a little Chinese, enough to follow some of her conversations.

"I thought pride was reciprocal," he retorted, because his father, the retired head of Linguistics at the University, withheld praise, having not forgiven the divorce. That failure, profound. *You shame the Pessoa name,* he accused in private. *What is Poetry without Love?*

"Not for Chinese sons," she responded, amused. Sonny was the same, after all, clumsy in his passions, ill-fitted, even now, to his half-Chinese skin. Yet this refusal to accept things as they must be impressed her, ignorant, as she was, of truth.

Eighteen years had not diminished their short-speak, although in matters of propriety, she remained superior. Discretion might have preserved his marriage. His American-Chinese wife reviled his infidelities. *You,* she accused when her tears had dried for good, *can go fuck your dilettante poet-girls. Your son deserves a real father.* His own eyes remained dry. Persona, after all, and a public titillated by the passions of fame. But that was before time played its tricks, exposing the lonely ache of his soul.

But now, in this present tense, the only imperative, the one thing he needed to know, was, "and you, Vicky, do you still paint?" No one else called her "Vicky."

Victoria was distracted. "Sorry, what was that?" Bruce Howell was leaving again. It was often his way, to forget, return and leave a second time. Usually, his antics did not intrude.

"Your painting. You must be able to afford a nice studio by now." *Howell,* he would later hear someone remark, *oh, him. "Art" for the rich and tasteless.*

§

A year before that night on the beach, he gazed across a desk into coal black eyes and imagined Victoria in his bed. She was reading his copy for her designer eyewear account.

"This is good," she told him. Their hands met briefly as she returned the sheet.

Sonny crossed his legs. "I have better."

"Show me." His gaze intruded. Her not-yet-ex-husband provoked less disturbance during intercourse.

"It's too good for ad copy."

"Why?"

"Because I'm a poet." He rolled his chair away from her desk — *propulsion* — and rose.

Her eyes devoured the curve of his hips. "I'd like to paint you."

"What would your husband say?" He pretended calm, but was betrayed by the blush of his cheeks. Two days earlier, he had overheard Bruce Howell utter at the urinal, *Victoria? I'd do her. She's too hot for that husband of hers to handle.* He hadn't dared but wanted to kick Bruce right then in the crotch.

She moistened her lips. "My husband . . . approves. He calls it my 'hobby' that keeps me amused." Stirred by the momentary freshness of her utterance, she declared. "All I want to do is paint."

"So why don't you?"

Startled by her lusts, she said the first thing that came to mind. "He would say I'm doing it to spite him," and blushed.

Which was why Sonny started to tell her his heart. To leave this city, to go write, to fall in love for real. *To fall in love.* He told and told, while posing for her, and she listened, while capturing body and soul.

Two months later, Victoria Chang and Bruce Howell became an "item." Sonny waited another six to bed her, which she allowed when she knew he would be discreet.

§

"Your painting," he repeated, sensing inattention.

"The paintings? Oh, those. You needn't worry. I painted over your poses years ago."

"No," he said, slightly stunned that she could have destroyed them. "Do *you* still paint?"

"Oh, *that.* Now and then. Bruce is the painter. I haven't much time, you know." She was impatient for her husband's departure.

§

A month before that night on the beach, he flung the proofs of his first chapbook at her and fumed. "He says I shouldn't go to America, that I'm wasting my time with poetry."

Victoria was put out by his unexpected visit that evening. She leafed idly through his volume, *The Science of Love*. Sonny was proving tiresome as a lover, more so as a poet, and she did not entirely regret his departure. "You need your father's blessings."

"Or his curse. He says I ought to write in Chinese."

"It is your mother tongue," she said, in Chinese.

"*Et tu?*"

Despite her protests, he forced himself on her right there, and apologized afterwards, ashamed of his anger. "I didn't know how good I was till now."

She lay on the desk, exhausted, her eyes half shut. "Oh, trust me, you're good." Her almost-ex husband would be by in less than an hour.

He tugged at her long hair, marveling that her mascara hadn't smeared. "I was talking about my poetry."

In answer, she pushed him on his back to the floor.

My light, my path, he whispered afterwards. *Give me strength for my art.*

In fall of that year, he left without his father's blessings. His letter to Victoria, written that winter from New York, also read, *Love plays memory for a fool but I strive to rise above that. I am determined to be The Poet; that is my rightful destiny. It would be best if you do not reply. I don't intend to see you again.*

When she did not reply, he had broken down and called. Bruce Howell answered, and Sonny hung up, furious.

§

"You don't paint at all?" Having imagined a finer path, he was humiliated. To have wasted love, even then, on a dilettante!

"Time marches on," she replied, meaning to continue the conversation, trusting he would understand. She watched her husband close the door, only to open it again and remind her of some inconsequence.

Sonny became distracted. "Time isn't money, you know," he quipped, wanting to hang up, now. Another face loomed: his wife in love, in tears. *Coward,* she accused, but he shut her out, unwilling to hear, while treading a path to regrets.

"Such a wit." Bruce having left at last, she could concentrate for the moment. Her voice turned dreamy and she said, in English. "It's been a long time, hasn't it, Sonny?" Saying his name conjured tenderness. His absent voice invited romance. "I haven't forgotten our beach," she continued. "The moonlight, the waves, the rain."

§

That night, clouds threatened rain. Lie as still as you can, she commanded. Reciprocate. He hung on while she gorged herself, and when she, spent, provoked his turn, he howled, in gratitude, at the absent moon.

Time stopped, trapped in that howl. He chafed at all women to come, unforgiving.

§

"It was a long time ago, Victoria." Escape! He had left her once.

She had not left, but her guilt belonged to other sins. "You'll see me while you're here, won't you?"

"You and . . . Bruce? Perhaps after Macau," he replied, adding, "I'm going as a Portuguese son." His laughter disguised the uncertainties he felt.

Her voice sank to its seductive alto. "Why not just me? This afternoon, perhaps?" Desperation underlined her plea. These moments were all she had.

"You're married." There, he'd ended it.

"That never stopped you." She wanted, no, needed, this game of love. Her nights were plagued by Bruce's snores, exhaling the weight of success.

Closing his eyes, he repeated. "It was a long time ago."

She was disappointed, even a little piqued, but a Bali home loomed, with all its choice possessions. "We'll be away after you get back, I'm afraid. House guests."

"What a shame." He glanced at the photo of his son, who was young yet, only four. Surely there was time for another path. Time enough for language, life and art. For a less fragile future with fewer regrets. A path of easier love.

Victoria was already abandoning regrets. It was enough to have recalled the hour. "Then, perhaps next time. Don't be a stranger."

§

We are both artists, she had told him that night. It was her moment of splendor before destiny took hold. We will follow the path.

§

"I won't," he replied.

APOLLO KISSED ME

That morning, I went to the rocks. It was an easy downhill climb from the footpath. The sun shone on the Aegean. To not offend the villagers, I wore a tee shirt and shorts over my tiny bikini. But on the rocks, my flesh would be out of their view.

The noon sun was not as hot as in the tropics. I lay on the rocks for an hour. The brisk September waves tickled my toes. I had my olive oil.

A shadow made me open my eyes.

I have watched you, said the shadow, for many days now. Ever since the rains stopped and the sun began to shine again. You come to the rocks to read, at noon. I am from the village in the mountains.

He sat down beside me. His skin was sun broiled. He wore

only a swimsuit, and was too blonde and tall to be Greek.

The villagers call me Apollo, he said. Are you from the tropics?

I sat up, conscious of my smallness beside him. He could not be a villager, I thought. This island was too forgotten to contain the likes of him. He spoke, a musical stream of images. His voice caressed the tropics — he said he had been there to dive. I heard the undefinable mixture of accents in his English, and saw his concentrated gaze on my skin.

He talked at me for perhaps an hour, then jumped up without warning.

Come back tomorrow, he said, a shadow again. Our sun is perpetual. I will make certain you put on more oil tomorrow.

In the tropics, said Apollo, the ocean is always warm, I remember the waves were very high. The foam formed a barrier against the outer waters before the cresecendo burst on shore. You are not brown enough.

He poured the oil over my stomach. The liquid spilled down my thighs. It ran in easy rivers down my legs. Warm.

I want to go back to the tropics, he said. Every afternoon, I used to walk in the rains. My skin felt moist all the time.

He knelt down and rubbed oil over my stomach and legs.

Lizard skin. You have lizard skin, he said. It's cool and dry and flaking.

Dry Mediterranean air, I told him. That is to blame.

You look tropical, but you're not. You should be browner, insisted Apollo, rubbing the oil more vigorously. And — he jerked the elastic edge of my bikini top with his thumb — in the tropics, women don't wear this.

A prickle of gooseflesh awoke my breasts.

Tomorrow, he said, you will return to the tropics.

I walked, conscious of my breasts, to the rocks. Apollo sat there, his body moist from the Aegean. I stood, a shadow over him. He was not as brown as I, nor as tropical.

There are no bananas in Greece, he said. Why are you hiding your breasts? Nor are there any mangoes, or papayas. You've tasted all those, I know. Sweet and sour. Tangy. Did you bring your oil today?

The olive oil was sticky on my hands. He rose and took the bottle from me, and unfastened my bikini top. The pale blue cloth fell in a crumpled heap upon the rocks.

Apollo's eyes demanded my flesh. He felt my bare skin with his hands. Look, he said, pointing to the less brown flesh of my breasts, this is not yet brown. Don't you want to be brown all over?

The chilly Aegean tongues licked my toes.

The sun burns you if you don't love him, said Apollo, his fingers still remarking my unbrowned flesh.

I looked down at the swimsuit which covered his loins. And you, I asked, will you not be naked too? My lightest skin is darker than your hidden whiteness.

He turned away and looked at the sky. On tropical afternoons, even the rainwaters were warm, he recalled. I would dive in the mornings, before the sun was hot enough to roast my whiteness. The rains washed the sea off my body.

Salty and hot.

He leaned over and licked my shoulder. I pulled at his swimsuit, but his hand stopped mine.

Tomorrow, he said, you will go home completely. Blue cloth is unnatural on your brown skin.

I have waited an hour, but Apollo has not touched me. His touch has only been to dress me with oil, nothing else. I have spent each day in the sun with him. Each day until he leaves.

I wait now, for Apollo.

Do you remember the feast with the pig, asked Apollo. I know it was in the tropics, because the sand on the beach was too hot on my soles. He savored the memory, and shook the salt spray out of his long hair. His hands rubbed the dark gold oil over my now completely naked body.

It was noon. The roasted pig sat on the grave in the sunshine gathering dust. A suckling pig. The skin of the pig was crisp and oily like Peking duck. The dust stuck to it. There were people like you around the grave: Chinese people of the tropics. Making peace with the dead. Some of them had white skin, had hidden from the sun.

There was one grave, a very large tomb on the hillside. The feast on that grave was sumptuous. Perhaps it was a family grave, Or the grave of an important man. Do your ancestors have large graves? Did you also bring a pig on visiting day?

I don't remember, I said.

He stared at his invisible tropics and did not move. Then, he continued. After that autumn day of the pig, I saw a funeral in town. The mourners wore white. In the middle of this hall, there was a feast on the table. The mourners made a lot of noise, wailing. Would there have been a pig?

Perhaps, I replied. I don't know for sure. I raised my hand to touch his arm, but he evaded my touch.

Will you take me to the tropics?

His question startled me.

I want to be brown, he continued, to be as tropical as you. In Greece, I do not sweat enough. He rubbed my thigh, spreading the olive oil around. Your skin is warm here, he said. His thumb flicked the stiff hairs, which were shiny with oil.

On another tropical island, Apollo continued, I saw many colours underwater. We barbecued a fish of many colours on the beach. Bare breasted women walked by. They carried drinks. The sand was black in parts -- was it volcanic?

Perhaps, I said.

Why would anyone leave the tropics, demanded Apollo. Why would you? He leaned over me, a shadow blocking the sun.

They eat the pig, I said, with all its graveyard dust. Sometimes, the pig sits in the sun all day, so that it's warm at the end of the day. Then they eat it. The skin drips oil. Under the skin is a layer of fat. The oil runs down your chin. In the tropics, you sweat all the time. Your skin exudes a natural layer of oil. Your eyes are half open in the afternoons because there's too much food in your belly.

But people are content, he said.

You avoid the sun, I continued. Your skin creases in the sun. When you're thirty, you're fat, and on your way to your fifth pregnancy. The sun holds you at a point of easy passion. The dust and oil; when the motorcycles go by they raise a dust storm which clings to your skin. And the sea is tepid, always tepid. You never wake, never sleep. Your dreams are full of mosquitoes.

Passion, said Apollo. His finger circled my stomach as he said it.

Then, I continued, on Chinese death feast days, there's a din and a clamor as noisy as a funeral. You want the noise of the cymbals and gongs to stop because the heat makes everything louder.

The sun in the tropics is noisy, I said.

I climbed back up to the footpath, leaving Apollo on the rocks.

Today, I went to the rocks again. Apollo was waiting. He lay naked, his face turned towards the sun. I knelt over him, and rubbed the olive oil on his chest. My hand was warm against the clammy sea layer of his flesh.

Today, Apollo kissed me. Once. There on the rocks. The Aegean crept up the rocks, further than I had ever seen it rise. The water splashed cold against my skin, as cold as his caress in the sun.

Then, he rose, and dove into the water. I would not share in his nakedness. I did not want his body, offered cold to my touch. He swam, and I watched, a creeping chill around my toes. The sun shone brighter and hotter today, but its warmth touched only the outer part of me. I could not wait for him. I would not wait for him. He left his passion in the tropics.

Apollo swims still, adding weight to the heavy waves of the Aegean. I stand at the beach, away from the rocks, and watch Apollo, his chariot pointed at the foam.

Tomorrow, I shall leave the island.

In the distance, a graveyard feast. The dusty pig's crackle makes my mouth water. Apollo remembers what I have forgotten. A gong sounds. The noise of the cymbals die away, drenched by the sound of the sea.

WAH KIU

Prologue from the novel

She burnt me.

In the early spring of 1983, she dragged me out to the yard of her house in West Shampton, Massachusetts. I screamed my protests all the way, but she couldn't have cared less. All she did was scream back that she hated me hated me hated me. And then she dumped me, most unceremoniously, into a thirty pound metal garbage can, and set me on fire.

Well damn her. I'm not going to die on account of a few flames.

After all, I've lived inside her for over two decades.

After all, I'm her only child and always will be, since she's had her tubes cleanly sizzled right through.

After all, I exist only in her imagination, which gives her the power of life, but not death, over me.

§

My name's Roberta Gale. I'm Irish from Ireland, although she's also conceived of me as Irish-American and Eurasian, and I have red hair and green eyes. My pyromaniac creator is a thirty two year old Asian-American woman who lives in Cincinnati, Ohio.

Edit. Rewrite. That's not quite true. She's an Asian woman. She has an Indonesian passport. She wasn't born and raised in America even though she's well on her way towards becoming "American." A mere passport does not confer so enormous an identity.

Wait, I still haven't got it right. She's mostly Chinese. Okay so maybe she's got some Indonesian blood coursing through her veins to justify the nomenclature "Asian," but don't they all look alike anyway?

They? What do I know? I'm a wholly unreliable narrator of Western origin whose right to name her is therefore questionable at best. Let her country people name her for better or worse . . .

The Chinese call her *wah kiu*. Overseas Chinese.

In 1965, when she was eleven, she gave birth to me.

At first she called me "Dear Diary." It soon became "Dear Roberta," and then "Dear Robbie, Rob, Berta, Bertie." Oh yes, I was dear to her in those days when she lived with her family in British Hong Kong. Her parents had just returned from a trip around the world. Mum brought home a stuffed toy leprechaun. I think that was why she made me Irish because she knew nothing about my country, except for what she had read in fairy tales and story books.

But why red hair?! No one in Hong Kong sported such a peculiar combination. There was one person, though, who did. Lana Lang, Superman's other girlfriend. She had no patience with Lois whose hair was black and permed like every woman in Hong Kong.

And green eyes. She had never seen green eyes, except on cats, and the idea fascinated her. So green eyes it was. It was different.

At first, my life was simple. All I had to do was read. She wrote me letters chronicling her life's events, in English, her native tongue. She was happy, she was happy, she kept telling me. She had a wonderful family and life. Her family and friends loved her, and she loved God, her family and friends, and me. If truth be told, she certainly seemed happy enough. No complaints.

Except occasionally when a scream stuck in her throat.

"Dear Roberta," she wrote, "today at school the nuns were awful again. I wish they would go back to America. Why must they play favorites with the Portuguese girls? What's wrong with being Chinese? Why don't the nuns like us?"

"Roberta! I wish the Chinese girls would stand up for themselves! Why do they let the nuns treat them so badly? Why don't they ever speak up? Why am I the only one?"

"Bertie, I was wearing my Girl Guide uniform today and stood up and saluted when they played 'God Save The Queen.' My friend A wouldn't. She says she isn't British even if the British says she is. How strange."

Tsk, tsk. Angry young girl.

One day, she grew up and unstuck the screams.

That was when she tried to kill me.

Well dearie, Roberta won't die, will she now? All this burning of letters to Rob can't kill my spirit.

My storytelling spirit.

After all, didn't she bring me here to America where I can invoke the first amendment?

Here in America, I can tell any tale I want, and it will find root, somehow.

So burn me, will she? I will tell her story whether she likes it or not.

Because all this garbage can fire business is about her taking the fifth.

Shame shame. Piper's shame. Robbie Gale knows all her games.

§

Chapter One. At the age of thirty, she left Massachusetts and moved to Cincinnati, Ohio.

At the age of thirty two, she was tired of being *wah kiu,* of being "different," and more exactly, of exalting that difference. Until this point, it had never occurred to her to be anything but different.

The revelation struck her along US 50 west away from Cincinnati in her two-tone tan Ford Escort '82 — here she reflected that she did maintain that god awful "difference" by refusing to purchase a new car, although she had conceded to driving lessons and the legal license accompanying the act of driving (two tries on the maneuvering test, Asians *are* lousy drivers) — and on a drive without purpose because she had turned off the wrong exit.

She turned right on the road she recognized as leading to the College of Mt. St. Joseph, and stopped. Maryknoll Convent School, a brick structure gracing a hilltop in Kowloon, loomed in her memory. How was it that the nuns, so generous with names such as Philomena, or Agnes, or Barbara for their non-Catholic Chinese charges, could have overlooked her wholly secular English name just because her middle baptismal name was Mary? At least it was better than being a boy at her brother's school, La Salle, where some students emerged with misnomers such as Bartholomew Chan or Nathaniel Ho. Misnomers? She wasn't sure. They were no worse than the populist versions such as Elvis Yip or McCartney Wong. Swinging the Escort around, she headed for home.

These days, driving had become quasi enjoyable. Little more than a year ago, she had arrived in Cincinnati with her American husband, and realized there would be no way around driving. Once, in West Shampton, Massachusetts, their former home, she had been almost paralyzed with fear as she misjudged their car onto a grassy slope above a parking space. It had been a tricky maneuver, getting herself out of that, and the only victim was a small green car in the parking lot that suffered a scratch on its side, and she had escaped with more guilt than a hit-a-person-and-run driver. That had been the end of her illegal driving days, and, for awhile, driving altogether. But in Cincinnati, with its so-very-American highways circling the city stretching from south to north, and its suburban existence, she finally accepted the need to drive.

The trouble was, she knew, as she braked at a light, driving was so terribly American. Yet few people, except perhaps other "aliens," tolerated this paranoia of resisting, yet idolizing, things American. The light flashed green, and she accelerated. Just what was it she felt as an almost full fledged suburban driver in this all American city? Exhilaration? Intoxication?

Just about a year ago, a letter arrived from a Hong Kong advertising friend in response to her request for contacts in her job search: *Since I haven't the faintest idea where Cincinnati is, let alone how to spell it without referring to your letter, you can imagine I won't be of much help.* The terrible thing was that her friend was Australian, had traveled widely in Europe, Asia, the Middle East, and even visited America. In short, he was hardly the provincial sort. It was not reassuring to know that Cincinnati could appear such foreign terrain to him, especially since she proposed to make it her home for a time.

She arrived in the vicinity of downtown and wove her way onto I-75. No more mystery: take US 50 W to I-75 N and get off at I-74 which will say Indianapolis but you can exit right away on either Spring Grove/Elsmore or Colerain Avenue. The way home. Not bus number 208 to Broadcast Drive from the Star Ferry. Or Chater to Kowloon Tong on the "underground iron," Hong Kong's shiny subway. Either way, it was still Greek to everyone but the Greeks who would have called it Chinese, perhaps.

Almost home.

ESSAYS OF THE CHINESE, OVERSEAS

ON BEING CHINESE

WAH KIU WANDERERS
(1995)

The existence of *Wah Kiu,* or overseas Chinese, has long been a delicate problem for China in her relations with ASEAN neighbors.

The term extends beyond China's immigrants to Southeast Asia to encompass countless Chinese wanderers throughout the world. These pockets of displaced souls typically have evolved to create a culture that is more Chinese than anything in China, and at the same time, their relationship with their motherland is often fraught with ambivalence.

In Hong Kong, the decade leading up to 1997 has given rise to a new breed of *wah kiu* — Hong Kong Chinese who would hardly apply the term to themselves, yet who exhibit quintessential *wah kiu* characteristics: they out-Chinese the mainlanders, and their political status, in light of 1997, can best be described as unresolved.

I lived as an Indonesian Chinese *wah kiu* in Hong Komg during the '60's and '70's, and found it an alienating experience. The Hong Kong Chinese viewed *wah kiu* with pity and disdain. Yet when I returned to live in Hong Kong in 1991 after an eleven year absence, I was surprised at how much more like my own *wah kiu* family many Hong Kong Chinese had become.

As a child, I spoke English with a British-Indonesian-Cantonese accent, and did not know a "mother tongue." Today, many Hong Kong Chinese children find themselves in confusion about their native language. They speak fluent English with a Filipino accent, acquired by daily proximity to their maid, or they rattle on in Canadian English, the fallout of their parents' pre-1997 pursuit of a passport.

Meanwhile, to give another stir to the *wah kiu* mix, has anyone counted the increase in Eurasian births, the once denigrated *jaap jung*? Interracial marriages are more than the stuff of Suzie Wong-type fiction these days; my *gweilo* ("foreign devil") husband is just another among many *sai yan* ("Western person") spouses in Hong Kong.

These new *wah kiu* are not confined to East-West migration either. Intra-Asian examples abound, and they're quite different from the people who caused China's original foreign relations problems. My minibus dirver in Kowloon Tong exhibits an admirable command of Tagalog, and is besieged by a flock of willing tutor-passengers who want to know when he's moving to Manila.

Today's *wah kiu,* for all their sophistication, appear to be less willing to endure hardship in a foreign country than their ancestors were. Murmurs of discontent are drifting back from Asia and the West, and the discontent seems to stem from a yearning for the good life left behind in Hong Kong.

I have listened to Hong Kong executives on a stint in their U.S. corporate headquarters complain bitterly about every aspect of life there. They have even insisted on bringing their rice cookers, because the foreign food was so unpalatable. Yet these same people spent most of the 80's looking for a foreign passport, and the U.S. (or Canada or Australia) was at the top of their list.

The truth is that life abroad has a near-fatal attraction — awful and terrifying, yet seductive. The standard clichés about the quality of life in Canada or Singapore fall easily off the lips of these Hong Kong Chinese *wah kiu.* But the voluntary exile cannot be accomplished without upsetting the balance of their identity.

However "Chinese" these new emigrants believe themselves to be, they will be subject to increasing confusion. Whether we're talking language (who put the *putong,* meaning "common" in Putonghua anyway?), culture (Confucius or Canto-pop?) or political ideology (hands up, all you capitalist Communists), Hong Kong Chinese can hardly claim to have a clear-cut "Chinese" identity.

But true to the tradition of *wah kiu* everywhere, they will insist they are Chinese. I know that cry only too well. It provides a security blanket of denial and comfort in the face of a reality that is changing too rapidly to assimilate or fully understand.

BURNT OUT AMBITIONS
(1996)

"People only want to work five days a week. The other two days, they enjoy themselves, go shopping, visit the pagodas. I think this is not good. They should work harder." Except for the pagodas, he could have been talking about any of the "tigers." The speaker was a fiftyish former taxi driver turned tour operator, history graduate of Yangon University, fluent in English and French and one-time scholarship student at the Sorbonne. He was complaining about his countryfolk as we sailed along the Irrawady.

Why should the people of Myanmar, a developing nation that is now opening up to tourism and foreign influence after its long isolation, resemble those of the tiger nations? The banks of the Irrawady are dotted with thatch huts that house less wealth today than the squatters that dotted Hong Kong's hillsides in the sixties.

"People work very hard in Japan," my tour operator friend continued. "That's why Japan is a successful country. I've started studying Japanese."

"Five-day work week" is often the most desirable employee benefit these days when other benefits have begun to fail to attract in conditions of low unemployment. Medical insurance does not hold Singaporean employees hostage the way they do their American counterparts. Likewise pension plans, as 1997 draws closer, are little more than a "by-the-way we have one" aside for personnel departments in Hong Kong. Among the young and not-so-young in both these cities, what matters is a decent job, a reasonable compensation for one's rank, experience and industry, and that magic music-to-the-ears condition, the five-day work week.

Don't let the headlines heralding statistics at either extreme of the bell curve fool you. The professed self-actualizing desires of the extremely well paid who want "career development" or "job satisfaction" apply to a minority. The rest of Hong Kong's *da gung jai,* popularized in Sam Hui's song some fifteen years ago, pay lip service at best to these claims. The reality also is that Singaporeans can and do "rest" between jobs when they get fed up of the demands of a particular employer, with little damage to their job prospects. And the media highlights unemployment, while government spokesmen like to play down that minority extreme of the general populace.

On the other hand, my Myanmar tour operator may soon

be singing a different tune. If anything, the growing influx of tourism and foreign investment may in time turn Myanmar's five-day work week into the seven-day-work-till-you-drop mentality that all the tigers are supposedly famous for, and now actually consider "a problem." In Yangon, my travel agent's representative showed up at eight in the evening upon my arrival to deliver my tickets and personally explain changes to my itinerary, for which she was most apologetic. Having determined my acceptance of those changes, she proceeded to return to her office to follow up confirmations and assure her boss all was well. I doubt she was calculating her overtime. If anything, it was a point of pride with her to tell me that she was a licensed and professional tour operator.

In Hong Kong, I gave up on a well-known travel agency after days of inept planning during which the staff never bothered to inform me of anything unless I asked. The agency I finally used was good in most ways, but they did warn me to make "special arrangements" should I need to come by after six in the evening to pick up my tickets.

Some of the tiger people have, I think, begun resting on their countries' laurels of success. Along with the five-day week mentality is the growing trend, especially among the young, to believe they "deserve" their jobs and high pay scales by virtue of their birthright. I listened, amused, to a recent graduate complain about sending out twenty resumes (imagine!) before finally landing a job. Little wonder that young American and Canadian graduates, who think nothing of sending out 200 resumes and even working a 6-day week for the right opportunity on local terms, sometimes land positions that "belong" to locals, to the chagrin of local graduates. Also, in many customer service positions, Filipino and Malaysian employees, who seem to take pride in providing friendly, proactive customer service, are emerging in record numbers. Having endured surly Hong Kong shop assistants, and unhelpful and even hostile Singaporean telephone operators, I can't say I'm surprised at these employers' hiring decisions.

Being a tiger citizen embraces responsibilities. While many people do recognize this, enough others are inclined to forget how they got there in the first place. It has something to do with complacency, with a fizzling of the fire in the belly. No one will deny that improved standards of living, better job opportunities and pay, economic strength and the greater availability of leisure are rewards due to citizens of tiger nations who won success through hard work. Nor should anyone work till they drop simply for the sake of work.

However, a five-day work week might just be one of those markers along the path of forgetfulness and eventual oblivion. Tigers, I hear, do better when they're "burning bright."

Afterword: This trip to Myanmar took place prior to Aung Sang Suu Kyi being placed under house arrest, after which that country's flickering flame of tiger potential extinguished.

MULTIPLE MEANINGS OF BEING CHINESE
One "overseas-Chinese" life in Indonesia and Hong Kong
(2001)

" 'Marry your own people,' my mother always told me." For Christine Go, the problem was defining just who her "own people" were. As an "overseas-Chinese" girl born before WWI in Dutch-ruled Indonesia, her choices were limited. And as an educated, independent-minded teenager who traded cows in Javanese village markets, she did not meet many people she was willing to call "her own."

Christine was my spinster aunt Caroline's life-long companion. They lived together in Hong Kong and bickered like an old married couple until my aunt passed away in 1993, following which Christine returned to Indonesia. Their common language evolved into a kind of Indonesian-English; the one Chinese dialect they both spoke with some fluency was Cantonese, although their accent was obviously non-native. As *wah kius* in Hong Kong, which was what locals called the "overseas" Southeast Asian Chinese, they were almost a breed apart, and lived a life that was unlike the local Chinese who comprise 98% of the city's population.

In our "global" era, "Canadian" can equal "Chinese," in nationality if not ethnicity, and in culture if not blood. Yet Asia today retains much of the racism that divides even people of the same race. Christine's life, which spans most of the 20th century, exemplifies the odd balance of survival and discriminatory instincts among those who are themselves oppressed.

In colonial Indonesia, the Chinese were often the intermediaries between native Indonesians and the Dutch, particularly in commerce and local governance. "The Chinese," she says, "thought they were better than the Dutch. Yet on the other side of the brain, they wanted to be Dutch. Meanwhile, Indonesians called us *'belanda-belandaan'* meaning that we Chinese pretended we were Dutch."

The Go family lived in Purwerojo, a village in Central Java, where they ran a dairy and slaughterhouse. This gave them status and wealth. Dutch customers were amply supplied with cheese and milk; during the Japanese occupation, their family remained unharmed because they could provide meat to Japanese troops.

"The Chinese are difficult," her father asserted, when training Christine to purchase cows on his behalf. "They go round and round and think about things you never think of. Buy from the Indonesians. They give you a better bargain."

Years later, as a translator at the Indonesian Consulate in Hong Kong during the sixties and seventies, Christine was to encounter other distinctions. When visa applicants were processed, the local staff called out each group by colors — blue was Europeans (the terminology for all Caucasians), yellow meant Chinese and red was reserved for Communist Chinese.

She was sent to a Dutch Catholic girls school, the preferred choice for the elite Chinese. As a result, Christine is competent in Dutch, English, German, French and Indonesian, but illiterate in Chinese (she understands but does not speak Hokkienese, the dialect of many Southeast Asian *wah kiu*). Most of her schoolmates were Dutch. There were some Indonesians, mostly daughters of government personnel. The Chinese were the smallest group.

"The Catholics were more progressive in education," she says, "but they didn't subscribe to mixed marriages. None of the Chinese or Dutch girls wanted to marry Indonesians." Her mother's opinion was more forceful. "Marry Indonesians? What, do you want to go on your knees from room-to-room to your parents-in-law?" Among the high ranking Islamic Indonesian regents or governors, this apparently was a practice.

Yet she herself saw something else. "Boys had full Chinese names, but we girls were only 'daughters of Go'. I didn't want an arranged marriage. I wanted to be the one daughter to keep her father's name." Christine never regretted this decision not to enter the "marriage market" as she calls it. Perhaps she was remembering the cow trade she knew so well. In her more reflective moments, however, she says she was the only daughter with a "non-Chinese appearance" in the family. "I'm dark and ugly, and have a flat nose." She had suitors, nonetheless, but knew it was because of her father's money.

The remarkable thing about Christine is her lack of self pity. In politically correct Western societies, many with less cause trumpet their victimization, wearing it as a badge of honor. Perhaps it was due to her living in Asia where discrimination and divisions are tolerated, even encouraged. After WWII, she came to Hong Kong with my aunt, and took her language skills to an administrative career at the Indonesian Consulate from which she refused to retire, until forced to, when almost eighty.

Christine had been a teacher in our family's home in Tjilatjap, a village near her own, where she tutored my other aunts. Caroline attended boarding school in Singapore, and they met when she came home on vacations. "I liked Caroline right from the beginning. We were both not pretty so we're quite okay together. When we met, I decided, I can handle this one." She laughs as she recalls her younger friend. "Caroline didn't want to remain in Tjilatjap. She said it was too old fashioned and people couldn't get as much education as in Hong Kong. I found it hard to decide whether or not to go with her at first, but I trusted her and told myself, if she can why can't I? So I went."

In Hong Kong, she was to acquire another moniker, "*jaap jung*" meaning mixed breed, a pejorative used by local Chinese for Eurasians. "I was always a foreigner there," she says, despite her residence of over forty years. "But I'm glad I went."

As a child in Hong Kong, I loved Christine like family. She used to spin tales about a girl called "Black-socks-and-white-shoes." "Why did she wear that?" I'd ask. "Because she wanted to," Christine would reply. "Now listen, this girl climbed trees, ran around, played with and even led all the boys when her daddy wasn't watching. During her period, she even swam, although she was told not to. She did whatever she liked, even smoking cigarettes." Here she would take a drag on her filtered Kent, the brand she smoked from the time I first knew her until her seventies, when the doctor made her quit. "Anyway, whenever Black-socks-and-white-shoes did anything naughty, she never got caught." She narrated this part with an air of great satisfaction. "Never?" This idea thrilled my six-year old self. "Never," Christine declared. It wasn't till I was older that I realized she was talking almost entirely about herself. The only piece of fiction was the footwear.

Hong Kong proved the place Christine finally chose to do what she wanted. Being Chinese or Indonesian was moot; what mattered was that she and my aunt lived a long and happy life together without interference. They both had careers, were able to travel, saw "exciting and new things," a bigger world than would have been open to them had they never left home. It was the path of her ancestors, the Go's who sailed from southeastern China many generations earlier to the shores of Indonesia. Even her family's secret no longer signified: a great grandfather had taken a second wife or mistress, a Eurasian, with whom he had several mixed-blood offspring. This outcast branch banished themselves to Holland, although their existence was whispered about throughout her childhood.

She attributes her independence to her mother. "I think I was her favorite," she says, "because I was the only girl who had something to say." Her mother came from a poor family who struggled to build their dairy business. Christine learned that her desire for independence would only be gained through hard work. When she approached her parents about leaving Indonesia, the argument that won was that "in Hong Kong, I can earn more." Besides, Christine's future in Indonesia was limited to teaching; despite her commercial abilities in the cow trade, only her brothers would inherit the business.

The multiple meanings of "Chinese" in Christine's life reflect her particular experience in Asia's historical evolution. Ironically, it was in British Hong Kong, the colony that never gained independence, where Christine felt most free. "I am Indonesian, not Chinese," she used to say of herself there. "Well, that's what the locals say." And then she laughs, because her time in Hong Kong was unfettered by anyone's conventions.

In yet another twist of fate, the girl who wanted to keep her father's Chinese name by not marrying was forced to adopt an Indonesian one in 1968, a result of the anti-Communist wave which affected Indonesian citizens of Chinese descent. Yet she almost never refers to herself as Christine Gondokusumo, except in banking or legal matters. She is Christine Go, the daughter of Go Wai Tik, the man who taught her to trade cows for profit.

In 2001, the year that the chronologically accurate call the real millennium, Christine Go turns ninety. She does not have much more of a corporal life ahead, and her mental life is slipping slowly into the zone of old age, although she can be remarkably lucid in conversation. I ask about freedom of choice and the meaning of majority opinion, since her life strikes me as one where choice and an unwillingness to buckle to convention led to a kind of fulfillment.

"Choice or your own opinion only matter," she claims, "depending on environment or circumstance. You can't change environmental opinion. I know my choice not to get married was right. You have to look out for yourself. The only thing is, it's not really necessary to be against anyone.

"Look at me, I have this ugly brown skin. Only who says brown is bad? Or like the nuns who baptized me when I was young. I didn't have to choose. Were they right or wrong? I don't know. I don't even know if there is a difference between 'right' and 'wrong'.

"The Dutch have an old saying, 'in de stade haven,' meaning 'may we arrive in the correct harbor' or, in other words, that things may work out. You can't change those things that happen to you, just like you can't change opinions of those around you. All I know is that because I do choose, I've done what I like."

Fighting words, while accepting the vagaries of fate., from this one "Chinese" life

Afterword: Christine Go died in the summer of 2001, shortly after her ninetieth birthday.

IF LIFE IS TO WRITE

ROCKING THE SAMPAN
(1999)

"Why don't you write in Chinese?" This question gets asked when I've given readings and talks everywhere, but most often in Hong Kong, usually by an ethnic Chinese, sometimes with open hostility. Inherent in that is the central dilemma of writing fiction in English as a mostly Chinese person from Hong Kong. "Mostly Chinese," my first cop out answer.

My Hong Kong origins seem to demand that I answer the question. Why write in English, why not in Chinese? 97% or more of Hong Kong's population has Cantonese as a first language. Yet Hong Kong is an immigrant city. If you listen hard to local speech, you'll hear Shanghai, Hakka, Chui Chow, Fukien accents and meanings. These days, you'll hear Putonghua tones. But it's all Chinese, right? The written language is the same.

Let's kill that myth. Hong Kong Chinese, the popular living language, includes a whole set of simplified characters that mimic Cantonese speech. This has little to do with the simplified Chinese of the Mainland. It also includes words like "fit" and "wet" written in English, which only marginally resemble their English counterparts in meaning.

And for a novelist observing society, the spoken language is paramount. Hong Kong people speak a brand of "Chinglish" that has found its way to Vancouver, Sydney, New York and London, into Canto and even Mando-pop, into movies and television. This dialect or language borrows from English and other Western languages as well as the English spoken in Singapore, Manila, Japan and elsewhere, testament to the city's global character. Whenever I render contemporary Cantonese speech, I find that American slang works well to capture its spirit and meaning.

Should being Chinese demand language define authenticity? In Canada or other English speaking countries, the idea of an ethnic Chinese writing in English is not unusual. In Hong Kong, however, the insinuation is often there: that a "real" writer from these shores wouldn't dream of writing in English. In fact, I've been told I can't possibly say anything real about Hong Kong because I write in English.

I'm a child of Chinese-Indonesian immigrant parents from Java, and was born in and have lived most of my life in Hong Kong. My parents spoke Javanese and Mandarin, and made English, which they had both studied, my first language for pragmatic reasons. So there's my second cop out — English, or rather ESL (English as a second language) is my "mother" tongue which is why I write in English.

It's time I stopped copping out in that polite, don't-rock-the-sampan, Hong Kong fashion. After all, any novelist knows that the wonderful magic of creating a fictional world is to uncover universality in individual experience. Language is merely a tool. While it might be slightly daunting to write fiction about Hong Kong in Swahili, that's not to say it can't be done.

As a writer, I love my Hong Kong heritage. It takes me down untrodden paths to create linguistic and cultural fictional realities. It lets me capture my slice of a landscape and people I know well. So in answer to those who must ask that question, I offer this untranslatable Hong Kong Cantonese slang — *you bore me into a muscle cramp* — which is about as "authentic" a Hong Kong answer as they're going to get.

WORDS AND THE CORNERS OF SOULS
(2000)

In a fit of "Fair Lady" pique, Eliza Doolittle sang, "Words, words, words, I'm so sick of words." The once illiterate flower girl had turned on her master, and a baffled Henry Higgins retreated, unable to comprehend her frustration.

Writing and reading are about the pleasure and power of words. The business of writing, however, calls for opening veins and dripping on the page to eke out something akin to truth, only to have some agent or editor impose commercial considerations that have nothing to do with truth. In literary fiction especially, publication and readership are not readily assured.

Having abandoned a life (and retirement)-sustaining career a couple of years ago in favor of a precarious writer's existence, I cannot help but question the wisdom of my insanity. There are days that Nicholson's fate in "The Shining" feels like an inevitable outcome.

Besides, no one reads anymore, or so say literature teachers, frazzled editors, disgruntled writers and those convinced that our electronic world is evil incarnate.

If I truly believed this, I would stop writing this instant.

It's not that I haven't felt this way myself. In my former corporate life, writing was reduced to one-paragraph emails or memos. College freshman, corralled into my section of a compulsory writing course, turned in "thoughtful" essays on "How to Drink a Bottle of Beer." And well-meaning friends buy my books but may never even make it past the signature page.

PEN's American Center recently invited me to speak at the Chinese Mutual Aid Association in Chicago as part of their "Readers & Writers" series. The Chicago group runs literacy programs for Chinese-speaking adult immigrants, and wanted to use one of my books as a text for their advanced students. It was an unusual request. Generally, I am asked to speak to literature and writing students at universities or colleges as well as at literary, arts or professional forums. This was my first time facing an audience that would have neither a native language nor high level of English literacy.

The business of writing assumes literacy. Yet all these "words, words, words" can mean little when literacy, especially for adults, is an added burden in the struggle of fitting into a new environment. While preparing for the talk, I couldn't help wondering if the desire for literacy among these immigrants had to do with a need to read much beyond signs and instructions or to pass the citizenship test in their new country.

Their program coordinator seemed extremely enthusiastic. She had selected *Danny's Snake,* my novella about an extra-marital attraction between Rosemary Hui, a foreign student from Hong Kong completing her Ph.D. in ESL education and Danny Leyland, a White American college student of Chinese who is a jazz baritone saxophonist. Rosemary's husband is Chinese, also from Hong Kong and a former jazz drummer; they are applying for their green cards. Their story is set against the events at Tiananmen in June of '89. If nothing else, I decided, the subject matter might appeal to the students.

Yet I couldn't help feeling a tiny bit doubtful.

When I arrived at the Association headquarters in Chicago's "new Chinatown" (in reality an enclave for immigrants of many nationalities), I was greeted by the enthusiastic coordinator, herself a graduate in literature and a Chinese speaker who had previously taught English in China. She told me that some of the students had found my work too difficult, although others managed to read some or all of it. The immigrants were primarily from China, Vietnam and Hong Kong, and were generally from lower income backgrounds.

I gave my talk, during which I discussed writing and the cross-cultural experience as requested, and did not expect many questions.

Sometimes, there's nothing more right than to be proven wrong. The Q&A extended well past the scheduled half hour. Both the students and tutors wanted to know about symbolic meanings, language use, choices the characters made. One Beijing man pointed out that the title of my book, *Daughters of Hui,* could be translated to sound like the Chinese name for "Cinderella," and wondered if the fairy tale had provided inspiration.

At the end of the Q&A, a Korean student raised her hand. Earlier, she had surprised me with her excellent Mandarin, explaining that she'd lived in Beijing a couple of years. Her English was much more halting than her Chinese. Could Rosemary fall in love with a Black man, she wanted to know. I was taken aback by the question: it seemed so far out of left field. Yet as I considered my work, with its theme of interracial sexual attraction and the jazz landscape that colors it, I said yes, I supposed it was possible because Rosemary would have had exposure to a Black community through her husband's jazz life. This led to a discussion about racial divisions, particularly between Blacks and Asians. Someone said this probably had to do with lack of exposure more than anything else.

Any writer's words, once read by another, take on a life of their own. I do not know what prompted her question. All I know is that something in my words reached into this reader and raised it. Another might dismiss such an observation, arguing that nothing in the text justifies it. But literature echoes the universal, regardless of specific race, religion or politics; also, readers bring their own experience to bear upon any story. Her question stayed with me afterwards, because it was a testament to the peculiar power of words, brought home in the most personal way possible.

Walking by Lake Michigan the next morning on a brilliantly sunny day, I was reminded of another incident from many years earlier.

While in graduate school, I taught in a summer college prep English program for inner city, mostly Black, 11th grade students from Boston. The curriculum focused on writing. Standards varied tremendously: some were clearly ready for the challenges ahead while others would be lucky to graduate from high school. Although I had previously taught ESL foreign students at the college level, this was my first brush with low income high school kids. For some of them, standard American English was almost a second dialect, if not language.

In order to write, I've always believed, it's imperative to read. Trusting instinct, I brought the class to the English department's library, and stuck some poetry in front of them.

There was one boy who hardly ever showed up to classes. On the days he did, he was surly, non-communicative and unwilling to write much more than a sentence or two. He happened to show up on our library day. To his, "I ain't gonna read no 'pome'," I replied that was up to him. "But," I added by way of enticement, "it's really short." Reluctantly, he made his way through William Blake's "The Sick Rose."

> *O Rose thou art sick*
> *The invisible worm*
> *That flies in the night*
> *In the howling storm*
>
> *Hath found out they bed*
> *Of crimson joy*
> *And her dark secret love*
> *Does thy life destroy*

He finished the poem, and, after a moment of silence, said, "I know a girl like this."

The student might never know or care that Blake was writing over 150 years earlier, a "dead white male" of today's literature cannon that battles over political correctness. The poet's words had lit some corner of his soul. Words have the power to switch on thoughts and emotions, creating connections across history and experience that offer a deeper glimpse into the human condition. It's the reason I read, despite the moving sights and sounds that blast our global consciousness.

In my self-imposed confinement, I do sometimes wonder why I continue to write and rewrite. Meanwhile, the publishing industry lumbers at its glacial pace, meting out pennies and impersonal rejections, blithely battering the writer's ego. My words are an ink spot in an industry which turns supermodels into "novelists," pop stars into "poets" and celebrities into "authors," where the words that count are those in the contract for a multi-million dollar film deal.

"Mutual aid" really is what it's all about. That reader in Chicago, like my student of some seventeen years earlier, help me keep the faith — no matter how "sick, sick, sick" the business of words makes me — that the art of words will always have a *raison d'etre* to validate my solitary endeavor.

To complete the session, I read a short excerpt from one of the other stories in the book, a piece set in Hong Kong about two sisters who are separated by immigration. I noticed one young man in the front row following the text intently. He had not asked any questions during the Q&A, and I had thought he was bored. Afterwards, some of the students came to get their copy of my book signed, including him.

He said he was from Hong Kong. I asked in Cantonese how long he'd been in Chicago. His face brightened as he cited the exact date of arrival, some eighteen months earlier. He then said that he liked my story because of its "intimacy" — he could feel the streets and landscape of the city he'd left behind.

Why write, I used to ask my college writing classes to get them thinking about the process. I sometimes pose the same question in talks about the novel and publishing to aspiring writers. The imagined fame that seduces the uninitiated fails to dazzle anyone who has undertaken the slow and arduous task of crafting words to tell a story from the heart. For many writers, publishing provides little by way of support or sustenance. Sales ensure your being "out of print" while the marketplace lusts for the next, hot new "product."

Yet every now and then, some reader comes along who has been excited, touched or otherwise moved by what you write. And then I recall my own early reading experiences, when neither television nor play could tear me away, because the words on the pages transported me to another world, engaged my emotions, made me ask questions, caused me to think beyond the narrow confines of my present life to something larger.

Why write indeed? For myself, the answer has to be that as long as someone reads, there is reason enough to write.

LINGUISTIC EROTICA:
To Disclose is to Conceal
(2000)

> *What is that which the breeze, o'er the towering steep,*
> *As it fitfully blows, half conceals half discloses?*

The erotic quality of language begins in words such as these. I borrowed these words — lyrics from the second stanza of the American national anthem — as the epigraph to my novel, *Hong Kong Rose.* These words promised, teased, caressed the imagination. Like the play of the erotic, they disclose while concealing. They have nothing to do with sex.

I write to embrace this language I love. In any literature worth reading, "erotic language" should be an oxymoron. If the language of a story or novel fails to excite the imagination and senses, doesn't it fail as fiction? Don't we as writers have to massage our sentences, tickle our adjectives, coax our semicolons, unleash the power of our intensifiers. . . don't we have to raise language to its sensual peak if we wish to create characters, plots, places and points of view, in other words, the stuff of fiction? The very act of writing is erotic. Why else submit to the isolation and angst inherent in the process if not for its promise of private passion?

Yet language itself is not intrinsically erotic. When it is, the reader suspends disbelief and submits willingly to the literary seduction. It is Nabokov unfolding Humbert's perverse obsession, *Lolita, light of my life, fire of my loins. My sin, my soul*; it is Kingston revealing, *"You must not tell anyone," my mother said, "what I am about to tell you. In China, your father had a sister who killed herself"*; it is Lessing declaring, *The two women were alone in the London flat. "The point is," said Anna, as her friend came back from the telephone on the landing, "the point is, that as far as I can see, everything's cracking up."* These opening lines are erotic because they do disclose, but with an underlying promise of something half concealed. You descend into Humbert's world, you hear whispers of a China where sisterhood is suicide, you totter with Lessing's "free women" at the brink of their landing. These are sentences with souls.

How does language get there, to that moment of suspense, without the melodrama and cliché characteristic of "erotica"? We write of things sexual because of what they tell of humanity. Yet language that is blatantly sexual quickly falls flat, descending into the predictable and unexciting. The problem with true erotica is that it must meet the goal of its genre which is to titillate and stimulate the reader to some level of sexual excitement. In its least attractive manifestation, it becomes merely porn. Having occasionally crossed the line myself between erotica and literature, I have learned to edit out the sexual. A merciless castration. For language itself to be erotic, it cannot be merely sexual.

Intellectually, it's easy to write about sex. Writers like to distance themselves from such pedestrian, animal behavior. Alternatively, they ridicule or dissect it, wax poetic about its obsessive grip, or, as has become increasingly fashionable now, posit an indifference. Passion has become slightly quaint in our age when the shock value of sex surpasses all barriers. Cool contemporaneous! Beyond post modern is a belief in the make-believability of the sensual.

But how sadly frigid we, and consequently our language, will become. Let us not forget after all that porn and erotica survive, while the fashionable in fiction is indulged only for the moment. The literature we read long past its "use-by date" comes to us body and soul. It troubles to stroke language to fulfillment because it is born of desire. For language to be erotic, it cannot be merely polished. To achieve true luster, its sheen must reflect the truth of our messy humanity in all its sensuality, its disturbing, disquieting whole.

So we return to content, to the *raison d'etre* of a fiction. As writers, we are sometimes tempted to evade content in favor of language. The techniques of teasing out the erotic in language can be mastered and produced with flair and seeming originality. Yet life resides in content, in the big ideas of literature that endures. Perhaps our age is shy of big ideas. God died and we no longer know if god lived. The sexual revolution is a "been there, done that" routine whether or not we were there or did that. Vietnam was the war to end all wars so war, like everything else, is the root of all boredom. And language, bless its soul, has succumbed to dissection in thousands of writing programs and workshops, producing masses of polished words which can even be, intellectually at least, "erotic."

Erotic language may tease, but for it to linger in the imagination, it must speak to the heart of the reader and not just the intellect. Time and truth enhance language to its fullest power; it will not arrive there via the hurry up approach the publishing industry demands in finding the next marketable "writer" for instant fame. Content that embraces the spirit of disclosure — the truth seeking we strive for, not memoir-making — will more readily find erotic expression than content that make-believes. If fiction is written from the depth of our feelings, from the body and soul and not just the intellect, then its disclosure lends itself to the kind of erotic quality in language that disturbs and sends shivers to the loins.

Of course, an unabashed passion for truth can make language sensual, but not necessarily erotic. The other half, the concealment, is just as necessary. This sensory balance of hide and seek is rather like good sex; it isn't achieved prematurely. The flip side of intellectually erotic language is born of a need to "tell all," along with the requisite tedious self-justification. Bad enough in memoirs, worse when forced into fiction. No thank you, cringes this reader. Give me language that sings, that makes me long for the touch of a lover because I do indeed love.

To write is the privilege of playing with language. To read is the satisfaction of language playing with us. When the tension between reader and writer dances on without desire for end, then the erotic has blessed language for as long as the dance may last.

WRITING THE "WOMAN'S BOOK"
adapted from "Marchart" Literary Luncheon talk
Helena May, Hong Kong March 6, 2001

I promised to speak today about the "creative process." That sounds so arty, a little pretentious, don't you think? So let's call it what it is. I'll tell you how I wrote my latest novel, *The Unwalled City*, the one sometimes referred to as my "handover book." It's really the only way to talk about process, about what we call "creativity," which, for me, is to look at the beginning, middle and end of the writing of a novel.

First, the elliptical title of this talk. When asked for a description, I said. "Oh, Call it Writing the 'Woman's Book'." There are two reasons for this. March is Women's month, and as an ardent, if not militant, feminist, I like being a woman. The second reason takes me to the true beginning of this book, to the moment of its conception.

That took place on Good Friday, April 14, 1995, at 8:00 am, in my room at the Conrad Hotel. The reason I can be so precise is that I keep a journal or log for every novel I write, in order to track its progress, record plot ideas, character descriptions, an overheard conversation to use as dialogue, feelings about a place, bits of research as I work.

You might ask, what was I doing in that hotel room? I was working for Federal Express then, living in Singapore, and was on a business trip to Hong Kong. So basically, I was playing hooky, starting a novel instead of doing my job.

But why a "woman's book"? The handover is not, after all, purely a woman's concern. Well, when I wrote the first lines of the book, I wasn't necessarily thinking "handover." Here was the original first line:

"It's a woman thing," she said.

You can search through all 309 pages of the published

version, and you won't find that line anywhere. But that same weekend, I spoke for about half an hour on the phone to my American friend Cathy, who lived on the island of Cheung Chau at the time. She originally came to Hong Kong back in the early 80's to be the french horn in the Hong Kong Philharmonic. Anyway, I told Cathy I was writing my "woman's book," about three, or perhaps four women in Hong Kong, from very different backgrounds, leading very different lives, the only tie being the common city,. Over the years, I have seen and heard so many Hong Kong women's lives and stories, I told her, and I wanted to make some sense of all that through fiction. And then I read her my first line.

Now is that any way to write a novel? I haven't the foggiest idea, but it is the way I write. I even had a title. Sometime earlier, I'd read a wonderful little book, *Einstein's Dream* by Alan Lightman, and fell in love with this one passage:

"Long ago, before the Great Clock, time was measured by changes in heavenly bodies: the slow sweep of stars across the night sky, the arc of the sun and variation in light, the waxing and waning of the moon, tides, seasons. Time was measured also by heartbeats, the rhythms of drowsiness and sleep, the recurrence of hunger, the menstrual cycle of women, the duration of loneliness."

Pure poetry. My working title became *The Duration of Loneliness,* with this passage as the epigraph.

Like my first line, that also disappeared from the book. What remained however, as I wrote the novel, was the measuring of changes, a rhythm of drowsiness and sleep, recurrence of hunger, the menstrual cycle of women and the duration of loneliness in the lives and loves for all my characters in *The Unwalled City*. There are three principal women characters, and one man. Poor thing. He was totally outnumbered.

So that's how It began. What I did next was . . . nothing. I was still finishing up my last book, *Hong Kong Rose,* which had to be turned in to my publishers. I couldn't focus on this new book, even though I was dying to write it.

As Virginia Woolf once wrote, so succintly, in the middle of a novel, "Time passed." *Hong Kong Rose* hit the bookstands two years later, and I breathed a sigh of release.

And then, on September 3, 1997, more than two years after that moment of conception, this entry appeared in my journal:

"Okay, attacking the novel. It's language that's bugging me. I will NOT write another in the style of Hong Kong Rose. *Bothers the hell out of me."*

I was grumbling about "point of view." My previous book had been told by a first person narrator. I was sick of the "I" and was determined to write from a third person omniscient narrator's point of view. In the creative process, this is probably the single most important decision a writer makes in starting a new novel.

Moving on to the middle of this process, I tried to figure out what I was really trying to say. I had a story to tell, about the lives of three women and one man who kept changing as they evolved. Names were a challenge, especially since two had both English and Chinese names. To "see" and "know" them was important. The man was easiest because I stole him out of my first published novel, *Chinese Walls,* where he had a supporting role. I already knew his name, what he looked and sounded like, what he wore, how he carried himself, what he did to irritate people, especially women, and his history. I think that's a reason why so many novelists write sequels, so that they don't have to re-invent all over again. Personally, I think that's cheating. When I re-use a character, it's because I need to know her or him better, in the context of new characters or situations. Writing a sequel is sort of like saying your last book wasn't finished. One thing about my process to date — it could change of course — when I finish a book, it's finished.

But back to these women. I could "see" two of them. The problem was the youngest woman, who was in her early twenties at the start of the book. For some reason, I couldn't fully imagine the physical woman. I had to see a real person. After one Saturday night out at the nightclubs, this entry appeared in my journal:

"The other night at Visage, I saw the artist-girl. She is young, at most 23 or 24. Slender and rather taller than I'd originally imagined her. Her face is worried, always slightly worried. She comes into Visage with a group of friends, all Chinese, but hovers in the background, on the edge, as if she doesn't quite belong. Her chin juts out — but the skin is smooth, quite fine and porcelain like. The kicker was the mobile phone. In but out, out but in, trying to reach someone or something.

But the clothes though of these 20-somethings! They wear bell bottoms, and ugly shoes. It's a pastiche of the 60's with disco at the periphery. And the strange return of polyester and plastic."

Well there she was, an early version. She ended up without a mobile phone, but the two older women carried mobiles. Hopefully, this gives some idea of what it's like to create a fictional universe.

So on to the handover, which wasn't the original concern, whereas what happens to these women was. Andanna, the young girl, is from a wealthy local family, and comes home from Vancouver, armed with her B.A. in music and a Canadian passport. Pretty much the first thing she does is move out of home to live with her musician boyfriend. He's from a lower income background and so isn't an ideal mate in her parents' eyes. Then there's Gail Szeto, who's Eurasian, forty-something, divorced because her doctor husband left her for a younger woman, his receptionist. Now she's a single mother who also looks after her own nearly senile mother. She's a senior executive with an American investment bank, so her job's high stress. *You know,* Gail says, *it's really hard to meet any nice, unattached men.* Finally there's Colleen. She's thirty-something, an Irish-American Sinophile, married to a Hong Kong Chinese businessman, speaks Mandarin better than her husband, and by the time the novel opens, even speaks Cantonese pretty fluently, because she's been here awhile. I'll skip Vince, the man, except to say that he's a commercial photographer and that the book ends with him, on the night of the handover.

What I discovered was that all these Hong Kong lives couldn't help but be affected by the handover, even though no one was a politician, historian, journalist, social scientist or China hand. In other words, they weren't folks who would pay any special attention to the event; they were just part of the milieu that is contemporary Hong Kong. The book opens in early 1995, so we're a couple of years away yet, but when I began the actual writing, the handover was already past.

That proved to be a good vantage point. All the media had disappeared, and I could sift through the debris and aftermath. I'd moved back to Hong Kong from Singapore in 1995, and my own experience as '97 approached got into all this. Let's jump ahead close to the end of the process, when a professor of English at the University of Hong Kong agrees to write an afterword to my book. I like quoting academics — everyone knows they're intelligent because they've managed to get their PhD's, while writers sometimes don't even finish college. Here's Bolton on the handover:

"Of course, it is true that for a brief while in the summer of 1997, a month or so, Hong Kong was taken over, but it was not by goose-stepping soldiers of "Red China," or the tanks of the PLA, but by the serried ranks of the international press corps themselves. They typically came here looking for a story whose plot they already knew, and the arc of their invasion ran through the hotels of the territory and the bars of the Foreign Correspondents' Club. In the event, the Handover itself was anti-climatic. Prince Charles came, attended the ceremony, and then he and the last British governor of Hong Kong sailed out of the harbor on the royal yacht Britannia. It rained a great deal."

I'm pleased he made this observation regarding my novel, because, in the process, I discovered many things about the handover, mostly what it was *not*. If this turned into my "handover book," it was because the event was inescapable, even though, on a day-to-day basis, it didn't really affect life.

But if I look at Andanna and her Canadian passport, or Gail, working at one of the many international banks that sprung up like mushrooms, or Colleen's Mandarin proficiency, which becomes increasingly more useful, I realize I am writing about Hong Kong's history as it happens through fiction. It's a bit inevitable for a novelist. Bolton says I write a brand of "social realism," meaning I don't write magic realism, historical or experimental fiction, but stay anchored in contemporary life and mores. And in Hong Kong, that includes the handover.

So that's where the book ends. I wanted to chronicle life, especially women's lives, during these years, because women's stories matter.

There is an afterword to all this. Over twenty years earlier, I wrote several pages of a novel that was never finished called *The Girls School*. There were three women and one man. It was set on an island in Greece, because Greece was my preoccupation then, as were all-girls schools.

Funny how life, and books, turn out, isn't it?

LIFE AS A "COLONY RAT"

(2001)

There were no scheduled flights to Red Wing, Minnesota. Instead, a flock of mosquitoes greeted my arrival, feasting on my blood. "The mosquito's our state bird," said the director of the Anderson Center unapologetically, as he showed me around the colony where I was to be one of three writers-in-residence. "They'll get used to you."

Here was the world of the artist in solitude. My novel-in-progress submission was awarded with a month in the country, where nature's bounty would inspire my senses. On my first walk down this path less taken — one evening by the river — bluebottles and mayflies invaded my hair. I fled to indoor safety.

During the past year, I've been a "colony rat" at three writing colonies or residencies, and head to another in

Norway this summer. The most recent — living in Jack Kerouac's Orlando home — lasted three months. Although residency terms vary, the basic idea of such places is the same: to provide a space for creative writers to do their thing, i.e.: to write.

For years, I'd written novels while holding down a full time job, envying writers who were housed and fed in these beautiful surroundings. I wrote wherever in between long hours, business trips and limited vacations, and slept very little. Now, having quit corporate life to write, here was my chance to indulge in that same "luxury."

The first night at Kerouac's house, I hardly slept. It was freezing. Admittedly, this was December, but surely the climate in Florida was supposed to be warmer than in New York? By five, I left my unheated home for the streets of College Park in search of warmth and breakfast. My promised food subsidy had not been ready the day before when I arrived, and in Jack's kitchen, the cupboard was bare.

Over coffee, biscuits and sausage gravy, I missed those mid-Western "birds."

The Anderson Center is the estate of Dr. Alexander P. Anderson, who invented the process for puffing grains. Place rice or wheat grains in a glass tube, heat the glass to just the right temperature and the grains will puff perfectly, not unlike novels inflating to a publishable length. Anderson's heirs bequeathed the center to the spirit of creative inquiry, as long as those inquiring were residents of either Minnesota or New York, a funding stipulation.

I got Mrs. Anderson's room (the couple apparently slept separately, we were told in hushed tones). It was beautifully furnished, the largest and only room on the ground floor. Every Sunday, visitors to the "open house" would rattle my doorknob, despite signs indicating otherwise.

Kerouac's house, by contrast, did not have a desk, presumably because he wrote under a tree. A desk appeared within a week, thanks to my nagging. Visitors rarely found the place — wonderful privacy — although that will change when the foundation installs a sign on the lawn. Being a newly established historical site and residency (I was only the second writer), there were teething pains. I stayed in the front section of the house where his mother lived since the back section he occupied was not yet renovated.

His ghost didn't hang out much, most likely because Jack preferred "the road," although I kept the 24-hour jazz station on to keep him company when he landed. It was the least I could do for taking over his space.

Despite inauspicious beginnings, life as a colony rat had its advantages. I feasted on more than cheese, broke bread and drank (probably too much) wine with writers and artists, made friends, gave readings, experimented creatively, and generally enjoyed my stays.

Sometimes, I even wrote.

LETTER FROM HYDRA, GREECE
(1981)

Dear Friends at the AWMA (Asian Women's Management Association),

Yasu, as they say here, from Greece. To those of you who knew me I am clocking in to say that I am still alive and well and struggling along in the management game. To the rest of the members, I am a former member who used to work in the advertising/marketing scene and one day dropped out of sight round about August, 1980.

There comes a point in every woman executive's life where she stops, looks around at her daily existence, and wonders to herself: what am I doing all this for? Men, mind you, have been doing it for centuries, as the process of self evaluation and life-goal assessments is necessary whether you play the management game of business, politics or whatever.

Women, however, have been playing those games for a much lesser time, although they were always in the scene as wife, mother, sister or lover. Hence, when it comes to that point in a woman executive's life, the question becomes further burdened by the thought: why aren't I simply wife, mother, sister or lover? Added to that is the fact that most of the men around her are also saying, *yes, why aren't you simply my wife, mother, sister or lover?*

We all know, only too well, the sleepless nights accompanying:

1. Will I get that job?
2. Will I get that promotion?
3. Will they send me on that management course?
4. Will they send me on that business trip/overseas assignment?
5. Will they accept my proposal?

Etc. etc., and above all, will they really believe I'm doing all this and still being a woman, and not some sort of imitation man?

When I began asking myself all of the above, and more, I realized that in this enlightened 20th Century, men are still having more fun in the management game. Women may perhaps be more capable, but men are still having the better time. About three years ago, I realized that if I was serious about playing the life management game, my personal circumstances demanded that I either pursue an MBA, or at least begin examining my likely career paths with the company I was at, or elsewhere. Answers to such question do not, however, materialize overnight. And I carried on working, attending AWMA meetings, talking to friends and colleagues in an attempt to find the way, or at least illuminate the path slightly.

Exposure to the business world does, fortunately, teach you to keep your options open. The option for me suddenly reappeared in my life around this same time, and slowly, persuasively, it began nudging its way ever so gently into my waking psyche. My option was everything the business world was not: romantic, idealistic, very private, totally impractical, unprofitable, low return on investment, and terribly sexual. At the same time, it embodied some of the elements of the advertising/marketing world I was in, because it was also exciting, energetic, high risk, fun, creative and totally sexual.

By now you must be wondering – did she fall in love, run off with some man and is now trying to justify her action? Well, two out of three's not bad. I fell in love alright, with a way of life and a long forgotten goal from childhood, which was simply, to write. And two years later, I did quit my job.

When I bumped into See Foon here on Hydra, I was still in the midst of living out my European existence and writing. When I bump into all of you in Hong Kong again sometime in July, I will be in transit and still writing. Writing what you ask? Novels, short stories, assorted bits and pieces and letters to the AWMA.

Let me assure you that this bit of life management I am currently undertaking is the toughest job I've ever had. The boss is a slave driver, pay negligible, and the hours impossible. And do you think I can afford a secretary? Certainly not yet. In the first eight months of this new "job" I've had to ensure that:

1. I could solve visa problems (try traveling in Europe on an Indonesian passport)
2. I could move a manageable size office and wardrobe.
3. Mail could reach me on the slow boat to Greece and other countries

Etc. etc.

But above all, I had to prove to myself that I could take all of this seriously without compromising myself in any way. There were days I said to myself, *girl, you must belong on the lunatic fringe.*

Happily I've made it so far, and have managed to chart a long term work sheet to keep me going at least for another 7 to 10 years, or until the next life-management crisis comes along. Revenue is deplorable at this stage: £35 in eight months would barely keep a cockroach alive. Yet I have already begun to see the real profit — I am finally beginning to really understand how to manage my life.

The spirit of the AWMA is obviously still with me, and seeing See Foon again, in my familiar-face-starved state was rather like encountering manna from heaven. I hope to see you all in July when I pass through Hong Kong. In the meantime, I am heading to Moscow for a few days, so I'll end, from Russia, with love.

ON COMPROMISE

adapted from **REMARKS TO THE KIWANIS**
Red Wing, MN, July 13, 2000

I am what is around me.

Women understand this.
One is not duchess
A hundred yards from a carriage.

These, then are portraits:
A black vestibule;
A high bed sheltered by curtains.

These are merely instances.

"Theory" — Wallace Stevens

I thought I would speak to you today about compromise, mostly because I've been thinking about it, but also because there seems to be something worth remarking about its nature. Compromise was a central theme in my last published novel, *Hong Kong Rose*.

To speak properly about compromise, I first need to tell a little something about myself.

I've been introduced to you today as a novelist, a writer of fiction, which is most of what I do these days. Writing is certainly my *raison d'etre*; it is, if you choose to consider the matter spiritually, why I guess I've been put on this earth. Of course there's also the reason of family, friends, travel, the cross-cultural nature of my existence — an ethnic Chinese-Indonesian from Hong Kong, but also, in the latter part of my life, an immigrant to this country. All that makes up who I am feeds my writing, and allows me, on a good day, to craft a few words that may eventually touch some reader in a meaningful way. At least, that's my hope.

But there was another life, quite a good life I might add, that I lived for some eighteen, non-consecutive, years. Up till the end of 1997, I also had a career in marketing and management at various multinational corporations. Since the Kiwanis is a business group, I'm sure you're all too familiar with the challenges of marketing for any business, and regularly face issues like — being creative about getting a profitable market share, through aggressive sales & advertising or strategic planning; the need to predict, as accurately as possible, next year's production and sales volumes, given all the probable variables, of the market, your work force, or customer demands which fluctuate like the weather — and then you hope that the fickle finger of fate, which pokes around commerce and life, will point kindly your way.

For several years at Federal Express, I would attend meetings with the Asian sales managers and we'd say — so hey, do you think Charlie will buy this forecast? And then we'd scratch our heads in Singapore or Manila, or wherever we'd have our conferences and figure out the best way to sell our targets to Charlie, or Fred, or whomever it was in our Memphis headquarters who controlled such decisions, praying meanwhile that Intel in Malaysia or Laura Ashley in Japan or any of our big customers wouldn't jump ship and go over to UPS, making us miss our targets.

That was one of my jobs. At other times, I also worked for

Hong Kong's airline, Cathay Pacific Airways; then there was marketing for Pinkerton's, the first detective agency in America, the job that moved me to New York City in 1986; I worked for a couple of advertising agencies; also a Wall Street law firm where my responsibilities included assisting at the funeral of our name partner, John McCloy. Some of you may be familiar with his reputation as an advisor to the US government over the handling of post WW II Germany. At the church entrance, our department secretary, a tall girl from Brooklyn, stepped — she claims, accidentally — on Henry Kissinger's foot.

In 1996, I decided to try my hand at managing the bottom line. That was when I accepted my final corporate job as the Circulation Director for the Asian edition of *The Wall Street Journal,* which, if you think about it, is just a fancy title for a paper route that happens to require airplanes instead of bicycles. Of course, I'd always wanted a paper route. It was one of those images of American opportunity I had, when I tried to picture this culture as a child back in Hong Kong.

But let's get back to compromise.

About those eighteen, non-consecutive years — I'd interrupted my marketing career for about four . I disappeared to Europe for a year to write novels and stories in Europe after which I enrolled in a MFA program in creative writing at the University of Massachusetts. I didn't resume the marketing track until after I'd completed graduate school.

I'd majored in English as an undergraduate, and also wrote bad poetry and slightly better fiction. When I completed my BA, I went home to Hong Kong and into the work force where the best paid jobs were in business. Perhaps it was naivete, the circumstances of my upbringing, the job opportunities in Hong Kong at the time, or simply a lack of vision on my part, but it did not occur to me that I could pursue a "career" as a writer of serious fiction, although I continued to write seriously enough on weekends, at nights, early in the mornings, on all my vacations.

When I was in my mid twenties, I published my first short story in a literary journal. I had also begun a novel. At that time, I was working for Cathay Pacific Airways as their advertising superintendent — one of those extremely colonial British titles — traveling a lot for business, loving my airline benefits, but questioning, all the same, the pull of my writing. What became apparent to me was that if I really wanted to advance in business, the MBA was the next logical step — at least this was what was implied by the likes of the *Harvard Business Review,* which I read on account of my job. However, if I wanted to be a serious writer, an MFA made more sense. It seemed like an either/or proposition.

What I question now is why artistic endeavors in our modern world seem destined to go in this either/or way. There was a time when the Vice President of Hartford Insurance wrote poetry — the American poet Wallace Stevens, one of our great modern masters. In graduate school, I met poets and writers who would treat all jobs only as a means to an end of supporting the writing, meaning the less job responsibility, the better. With the exception of teaching creative writing, the idea of pursuing a career seriously in another field barely existed as an option. Of my graduating class in the mid eighties, the majority that have continued most successfully as serious writers all teach creative writing at universities. Many who pursued careers in the so-called "real world," even those who were journalists or technical writers, seemed to have limited their own literary work or, in a few cases, stopped writing completely.

Somehow, I managed to live with the compromise of doing both.

I can tell you now — it was a compromise. The time factor aside — I believe that each of us makes time for what we really want to do in life — the business world I lived in made very little room for a serious writer, or any artist for that matter, except as a hobbyist. Likewise, the writer's or artist's worlds, whether in universities or among broader artistic circles, provided little room for someone who markets Federal Express or Pinkerton's, except to see such endeavors as the "necessary evil" of money, but certainly not that of passion.

Life felt schizophrenic. I got published, gave readings, exchanged and critiqued work with other writers, complained about publishers while schmoozing with agents and editors in order to get published. But that life was separate and distinct from strategic planning for Johnny Walker whisky, one of my advertising accounts; or establishing a desktop publishing division to produce newsletters for the Trusts & Estates practice at Milbank, Tweed, Hadley & McCloy, or arguing with Korean distributors over the costs of expanding our delivery routes in Seoul for *The Asian Wall Street Journal*.

For years, I thought of compromise as a curse. The word suggests a sell out, an inability to maintain a singularity of purpose, a wishy-washy approach to life. Maybe, the only reason I could tread both paths was because I wasn't all that good either as a marketer or a writer? Yet there was something defeatist about this interpretation which made me uncomfortable, even as I felt uncertain about saying, as positively as possible, that of course it was good to have a foot in both worlds because hey, that made life so much more interesting.

Unfortunately, that's a bit like saying how wonderful it is to be of more than one culture, the way I am, because you get the best of both. This may be true on one level, but ultimately, it is too pat a statement, too easy an idea because it merely scratches the surface of things.

To write well, to be any kind of artist, demands an in depth immersion in that process. But more important, it demands a search for a deeper truth about the human condition. Mouthing mere platitudes and complacently obvious ideas simply doesn't cut it.

In the meantime, if our democratic, capitalist economy is to forge successfully ahead in the 21st century, businesses and corporations need people who will grapple passionately with the changing technological and global challenges we face, people who are unafraid of change, who look for innovative solutions, who won't settle for the way things always have been.

To parphrase one of my former employers, Federal Express: There is absolutely, positively, nothing wishy-washy about either endeavor.

However, there is something important about the crossover

of these disciplines so that one need not exist at the exclusion of the other.

So let me ask this group, the business representatives of this community — when was the last time you truly reflected on a poem, read a literary novel, or looked at a painting, really looked, by which I mean not simply going to some museum to keep your wife or husband happy, or because as parents, you felt obliged to drag your children there?

Passion feeds passion. I have roots in these disparate worlds of the arts and business and draw passion from both. I do not think the two are mutually exclusive. Yet experience suggests that these worlds find far too few meeting points. I'd love to be proven wrong. My being here today is, I hope, a sign that there continues to be opportunity for dialogue because somewhere, someone cares.

The Anderson Center, where I am privileged to have the residency that brings me here, is a place founded on the principle of interdisciplinary exploration. It was with this idea in mind that I've said what I have today, and trust that these have been words worth saying.

OVERLEAF, LIFE

IF I WRITE ABOUT MY AMERICAN CITY

(2001)

Maybe if I write something, anything — instead of addressing the day-to-day preparations of flying again — that isn't yet another email about the madness of life right now. . . maybe if I write, I will be able to make some sense of my existence, which resounds, right now, more deafeningly than usual with the rest of humanity.

I was in Hong Kong on September 11th and did not return to New York till the 20th. Summer was spent in Norway, two months away from both my home cities, at an idyllic and peaceful writer's retreat. This year, the city to which I returned did not spark that old favorite song in my head, as it does each fall, "Autumn in New York."

My lover Bill and I walk through downtown Manhattan early

on a Sunday morning, a week and a half after my return. For days, I saw posters lining the walls of my city, the eyes of lost souls staring back at me. "Have you seen my sister, our colleague, my husband," they read. I was aware of space in the streets, where not enough people got in my way, fought for cabs, rushed through the hours with a familiar intensity. Through evenings, I saw empty restaurants and bars in my Chelsea neighborhood, where a gay community congregates, where many complexions and tongues fill the nights with laughter, where cash registers ring even amid a slowing economy. Every morning on the walk to my studio, I glanced backwards at the void where my orientation landmarks once stood.

I must steel myself to go there, early, that Sunday morning.

Already, people gather to bear witness, to gawk, to mourn. It is large, this aftermath of destruction, against the presence of all that military in combat fatigues, the NYPD and state troopers, the fire department, sanitation workers and Red Cross. There are barriers at many points. These are not the streets I remember from 1986, upon first moving to New York, excited over my new job at 100 Church Street, a building whose windows are now covered with a fine patina of dust, as all the windows of downtown are. Dust brushes our cheeks, stings our eyes, chokes our lungs. We taste the grit between our teeth. As my ex-boss Mimi, who confronts this daily on Wall Street says, her office has a view of a graveyard.

An hour later, we head north to Chinatown, where the usual Sunday bustle is muted. Further north, along 12th Avenue, a military convoy flanks the path to our storage space. Much of the west side is closed or detoured. A recently opened bike path, from the George Washington Bridge to the southernmost tip of Manhattan, is not an easy exercise road any longer. Men in black with guns emerge from unmarked cars to stalk the streets. We walk home in silence, confounded by our state.

New York had just started to look fresh and young again, with a beauty born of a renovated and manicured west highway, of clean subway platforms and stations, of brand new subway cars, of much less crime, of a continued boom in property prices. Giuliani's legacy.

Now, police cars from upstate towns patrol the neighborhood. Tomorrow, I begin my journey to the Pacific Northwest, and will look for the National Guard that Bush has charged to protect our airports. Future shock, already present.

What is it I feel? In the lyrics of Vernon Duke, "Autumn in New York" is heavily "mingled with pain" this year in a grotesque and bizarre spectacle. My American city is disoriented. People are tentative, somber. The talk at the next table of every restaurant is of this, this terrible moment. What else is there to speak of? Our favorite bartender John, an aspiring actor and playwright, begins speaking of baseball, but then tells us his younger brother is in the navy, shipping out.

And I wonder about those friends I have yet to hear from, who might have been there, who might be grieving for relatives or lovers or friends who were there.

How should life go on? What do I tell the students at Blue

Mountain Community College about the writing of fiction? What do I say when I stand up in Pullman or Seattle or Vancouver to read from my tales of Hong Kong, about my Chinese city's moments of man-made turmoil? How do I connect this raw, tense present to the time and space of my fiction? And when will I see what those 19 human beings perpetrated — because they were a part of our humanity even if I will never condone what they did — as the existence of that potential in all of us, to hate, to destroy, to engineer our own deaths and those of others for a cause we believe in passionately?

Isn't that why I write, to record the profane and sacred permutations of courage, shame, love, hatred, desire, passion, uttered in multiple tongues of this Babel of races we inhabit? Isn't that why I write, because it is a way of participating in humanity, the terror and beauty, this deep well of collective anger and sorrow?

Isn't that why I write, to tell the story of this era I belong to, before my time is up?

"HOME" IS WHERE WE ALL MIGHT BE
Radio broadcast December 30, 2001

Being a Hong Kong "astronaut" who shuttles between cities, I like thinking of home as where the heart is. This comforts me and feels permanent somehow, regardless of where I lay my head each night. Since September 11th, however, I've become ambivalent on that score. "Home" now feels like a land of perpetual impermanence.

I've lived in New York City, off and on, for roughly a decade. It's the one place besides Hong Kong that feels like home. Long before I set foot in that city, it was real in my imagination. New York was the ultimate destination, regardless of race, language, culture, sexual predilection, profession or social status. It was Mecca for those of us who dreamed of personal freedom.

But there's much I would not recommend about New York.

It's harder edged than Hong Kong, ruder than London, puritanical compared to Paris, and dirtier than Singapore. In the U. S., New York is not America. Its history is one of transition: you arrive in order to make it, and having made it, you leave.

New York stands alone, defiant and arrogant, and embodies some of the worst characteristics of the free world.

Before the towers vanished, no one, not even Bin Laden, imagined this possibility. We war mongering humans perpetuate destruction while clinging to our ideas of order in the quasi-permanent state of continued existence.

The day the towers fell, there was cheering in Kabul, anger in Washington D.C. and a stunned silence around most of America. It reminds me a little of Hong Kong on July 1st, 1997 (when the "handover" to China occurred). The colonizing British wept, the Chinese cheered and Hong Kong-ers were ambivalent about this return to the Mainland. It all comes down to point of view, to your sense of what constitutes "reality."

The remains of the World Trade Center on television conjured visions of the Parthenon. Yet as I walked around Ground Zero in late September, eyes stinging from the dust, senses overwhelmed by the scale of these ruins and my mind rejecting the presence of so much homeland military, what struck me was my absolute inability to be certain of how or what I truly felt. The events that followed have simply increased my sense of ambivalence.

Ambivalence is not generally considered a virtue. Perhaps it's time to rethink this viewpoint. In the wake of September

11th, certainty seems more and more like an exercise in self deception.

Confronted by my New York home today, I see impermanence in every place and people on this planet. Our global community has never been "home free." The annual flooding of the Yangtze River and other forms of natural destruction are compounded by profitable man-made destruction, and further exacerbated by the self destruction of societies, families and individuals.

Which New York sings to me now? Sinatra's forecast feels too certain: if you can make it there, you might not make it anywhere. Vernon Duke's "Autumn in New York," so "often mingled with pain," feels too immersed in a history of despair.

These days, I take comfort in Billy Joel's "New York State of Mind," a tune first heard in Hong Kong long before I lived in New York. It speaks to a yearning anchored in a continuous present. Seek and you too shall find the path home.

Year end is usually the time for past reflection and future optimism. This year, things have changed. I cannot claim to speak for the world, but I suspect I'm not alone in my need right now to make sense of the present instead.

So this year end, in thinking about "home," I seek solace from impermanence and yearn for the power of dreams and imagination. In dreams, said Delmore Schwartz, begin responsibility. And through imagination, all the best possibilities can be real if we so choose.

AMERICA'S FACE
Radio broadcast November 26, 2002

There's a new complexion on the face of America. In recent times, there's rarely the blush of embarrassment or apology.

America is, in a word, afraid.

Fifteen years ago, I pledged allegiance to the flag at the age of 33. As an adult, it was a conscious choice to "sign on" to this superpower, this land of the free and home of the brave. Over the years I've traveled on the blue passport that allows such ease of access around the world, grateful not to have to queue on Garden Road for a visa.

Since 9-11, I've flown often both in the U.S. and internationally. The overwrought security at airports has given way to an unapologetic routine. What astonishes me most is how all travelers, and especially Americans, surrender to this new reality.

Fear does funny things to people. Some run and hide, abandoning New York City for the safety of the suburbs and rural hinterlands. Some engage in denial. Under the spacious skies, there are folks who appear not to hear the drumbeats of war. Others wear agony on their sleeves, as if perpetual hand wringing over the state of things will make our troubles go away. Still others turn their faces to prayer, begging deities to eliminate the horror of uncertainty.

If you cannot know for sure, isn't Ignorance the supreme commander?

Our commander-in-chief wears the most unembarrassed face of all. Perhaps it is ignorance, the bliss of one who has never suffered either slings or arrows. Fear has no room for compromise – be with us or against us – because we don't know what else to do and are too scared to discuss the issue. Or perhaps it's an inability to acknowledge fear, and bravado suffices where true courage fails.

But the bully will lead our global schoolyard so long as others follow.

A perpetual blush colors my American face right now. The rants of citizens of other nations make me angry at my own nation, this rich country that has so much, that is so privileged, that barricades itself in splendid isolation, refusing to understand how much of the world despises us yet feels compelled to follow.

It makes for an uneasy, national belonging.

In July, I sat on the floor of the Los Angeles airport, hunched over my laptop, waiting for a connection to Auckland.

Reminiscence over the travels of my younger days led to the following observation — When did airports become such noisy, uncomfortable places? They used to be places of infinite wonder, and humming, not noise.

Yet if romance has vanished from travel, does the fault lie with the airports, or the traveler?

There's a new grandeur on the face of the airports in America that I've only recently begun to see. Detroit's construction is finally completed, and this hub can now handle its heavy traffic exchange. Seattle is catching up, apologizing for its inadequate face, with a promise of a new look soon. At JFK International in New York, new construction takes its lead from Amsterdam's Schipol, one which has long catered to global crossings. Even Newark, New Jersey has finished its face lift, and we no longer mock its claims as an international center.

And the airports are safer, immigration and customs less ignorant, security more competent. Airports are now better poised to embrace the true meaning of "globalization," one that takes into account the changing movement of people and their dreams, so that less baggage is lost and more dignity reclaimed.

Being Chinese, I ought to believe in face.

Perhaps if I hold onto the romance of airports — and democracy — the blush will eventually fade. Faces that command come and go. But that continual, unstoppable global migration ensures that other faces will emerge, so that fear need not always be America's face.